The Book of Saints

The Book of Saints

A Novel

ROSANNA OGLE

THE CHOIR PRESS

First published in the United Kingdom in 2024 by
The Choir Press

ISBN 978-1-78963-422-8

Foreword

I've always disagreed with banned books and writings. When books are banned or burned, regardless of their content, it's usually a sign of oppression. Had I not been in the University's library at that specific time I wouldn't have known any books there were forbidden. The head of Theology and one of my lecturers had walked in shortly after me. They spoke in hushed tones with the librarian at the desk. I was between bookshelves so I can only presume they hadn't noticed my presence. The library was otherwise deserted as it was late in the evening. I didn't catch the whole conversation but it was apparent that the document in question would be put into storage and never released to anyone under any circumstance. What I did next was not like me, despite my disapproval of the censorship of the written word. I don't know why I took it, but I saw the opportunity when the librarian walked away from the desk to put books back on the shelves and slipped it into my bag. The lecturer had been very clear that the librarian should put the document in storage immediately. This might have been why my theft had gone unreported.

When I first began to read this document, I realised it was a translation of an original text that was in Latin, with possibly some Spanish or Catalan. It was not immediately clear why it was headed for the vaults, but my initial guess was that it was due to its unsavoury account of how Christianity was established in Britain. I was unsure of how it came to be in the hands of a lecturer of Theology in Paris. I also wondered where the original document resided (if indeed there was an original and the whole thing was not faked). As I read on, these questions began to burn for answers. I decided to research and put my findings into a small publication, though more as a curiosity than a serious academic work.

My mother used to say that we should never eavesdrop on conversations because one day we might hear a conversation about ourselves, and nobody wants to know what others really think of us. She was right about not eavesdropping, but she couldn't have guessed the repercussions of hearing a private conversion in a library. I've refused to go to the doctors with my Anxiety despite heart palpitations and panic attacks persisting and increasing. I don't want to take the kind of medication they drug housewives with, something that will put me in a trance. I don't want to lose my alertness or touch on reality any more than I already have. Maybe eventually I will experience full psychosis and they will lock me up and I will have no choice but to take the medicine they give me.

Marguerite M Martin
Paris 1952

Introduction

This book was dictated to Gueraula de Codines of Castile at the Tinkinswood Burial Chamber in the Vale of Glamorgan near Cardiff in Wales between Midnight and 1am on three successive days, December 18th, 19th, and 20th in the year 1325.

The author claimed to be the peasant woman Tavia, a Christian nun and travelling companion of St. Fagan and St. Deruvian in the 2nd century.[1] Through Gueraula de Codines, Tavia told, in Latin tongue, the story of the journey of the Saints through Britain following a letter requesting baptism from King Lucius himself to Pope Eleutherius.[2] Tavia's reason for dictating her story was 'so that man would know the truth'. It seemed her spirit could not allow itself to rest until she had untangled the legends, mysteries, and facts of how Christianity became established in Roman Britain.

How could she prove she was in fact a spirit from the early history of Christianity in Britain and so entitled to speak about the saints in so brazen a manner? Clearly, she must show knowledge and evidence from this time that no other has known or possessed.

First she showed her evidence by relating the movements and actions of the saints in minute detail, describing a Britain long forgotten.[3] She also showed her knowledge by outlining events that were yet to take place in the near, middle and distant future, due to the actions of these men.

---

1. The only written documentation of whom is by infamous fibber 'Geoffrey of Monmouth' in his History of the Kings of Britain so we are off to a good start.
2. This exact story being from said History of the Kings of Britain.
3. It seems obvious that this could be achieved by any basic author of fiction.

By the use of the Enochian alphabet during some passages she expressed deep understanding of the universe and beyond, the study of which necessarily requires the highest human scholarship to interpret and years of discipline and application.[4] There is much still to learn from Tavia's story and still much to work out, but there is enough here to validate her claims; the most cynical intellect is forced to acknowledge its truth.[5]

To understand this manuscript fully, it is best to study under the supervision of Gueraula de Codines, whose blessed gift and years of contact with the spirits have led her to an existence that treads a path along the precipice between life and death. An existence that requires negotiations from both beings of light and those of darkness.

Despite this, much of the language is clear and no simple scholar versed in Latin could read this story without being both enlightened and sickened to the very core of his being.

Be warned, the knowledge given in this manuscript cannot be unlearnt. Those reading this dictation will also find themselves in the abyss between life and death. By the end they may find themselves in the arms of angels or quite as easily shaking hands with a devil.[6]

The comprehensive account of the events leading to this dictation can be found as an appendix to this book.

---

4. A quick flick through this paper disproves the presence of Enochian symbols though even if these had been included in the original document the Enochian system can be found in several occult texts (granted they may have been more difficult to come by in the middle ages if indeed this was originally written in the middle ages).
5. I beg to differ.
6. I'll take my chances.

One

There was a chestnut-coloured bookcase devoted to Bibles and Christian texts. The police, social workers, and Tabitha's mum insisted on the importance of the break Marguerite and the church had given her. You were lucky, they told her, had you vandalised the property of anyone else you wouldn't have been given a second chance. As Tabitha stood in front of the elderly woman's battered chair, head bowed, her gaze fixed on the swollen feet and ankles that matched the maroon slippers they'd been forced into. Above the recliner was a painting of the crucifixion. His face and eyes were upturned, mouth open and curved down in tortured horror. His body writhed and chest strained with gasps that revealed the arch of his ribs. Tabatha heard once that there'd been a lot of art done in the olden days where Jesus was painted with a death erection. The church suppressed it because they considered it obscene. The hairs on her arms were raised up on goosebumps and she shivered in her thin top. It seemed colder inside than out and the dark furnishings and decoration made it worse. Over the years of meetings in school with headteachers and her mother, meetings with youth workers and her mother, meetings with police officers and her mother, Tabitha had become an absent participant. Sometimes she rolled her eyes on the rare occasion she was addressed directly but would usually be elsewhere. The thud of the front door brought her back into the room and she was alone with Marguerite.

'That's better,' Marguerite said after a silence thickened the room. 'So it was you who wrecked my porch windows?' There was an accent twisted so tight into Marguerite's finishing-school-English it was impossible to unravel. 'I don't suppose you knew the saints you smashed into a million pieces?'

Tabitha shrugged as she slumped into an armchair opposite. She tried not to look shocked as it almost swallowed her.

'I rescued those windows from a medieval French convent that

1

was being demolished. It sustained a lot of damage in the War. I had them restored and kept safe for years until I bought my first home and could have them installed. Transporting them cost hundreds of pounds, even back then, let alone the cost for the restoration and fenestration.' Marguerite left a suitable pause for a response but Tabitha craned her neck to look out of the window. 'Well, you just don't give a shit do you?' Marguerite murmured before she rose to her feet with more ease than expected. She strode to the kitchen without a stick or a frame and left Tabitha in the company of a hostile grandfather clock tick-tocking obnoxiously in the corner. Other paintings hung on the walls of the front-room. Some were detailed and looked as close to the real thing as you could get. Others were random shapes clumped together or something like the form of an unclear naked body. There were also odd objects lining shelves, sideboards, cabinets, that looked like they had come from everywhere. Elaborate vases and pottery to eerie heads with matted hair or ornate bones and teeth. And everywhere else there were wolves of all types. Wolf masks, wolf ornaments, wolf skins, pewter wolf inkwells. Marguerite returned with two cups: a floral fine bone china cup for herself and a thick white mug for Tabitha which clunked onto a coaster next to her. Tabitha slurped. The tea was bitter and tasted harshly of tannin.

'Could I have some sugar?' she asked.

'Don't have any,' responded Marguerite and sipped her tea before she added, 'besides, it seems you're sweet enough already.'

She didn't know why she'd smashed those windows. She mightn't have lived with much of a moral code but vandalism wasn't her usual modus operandi. That night she'd been at The Dusty Forge with her boyfriend. They'd decided not to go into Cardiff town centre because they were drunk already and there'd been a push by pubs and clubs to deny entrance to people in this state. This would leave the pair of them angry and out on the street where they would get into fights with any passer-by or – most commonly – each other. It was these fights that earned her a reputation with the police and led to the criminal behaviour order which resulted in her compulsory attendance at Marguerite's house. Despite not going into the centre of town that night, Tabitha and Tyler ended the evening standing on the pavement screaming at one another. In simple terms the argument had started after Tabitha had spoken to another man in the pub. However, there was a cloud of toxic fumes around the pair most of the time and Tabitha wanted to light the match. A few days before, Tyler had hit Tabitha bruising her cheekbone. This came after weeks of promises that it would never happen again. The first time he'd done it had been more than a sore face. It wasn't long after they had moved in together, at the protest of her mother. Tabitha hadn't left the flat for two weeks so the neighbourhood wouldn't see and report back. After that time the subsequent attacks seemed like love-taps followed by a day stuffed with doting, promises, and apologies. This latest punch had come without recompense though and Tyler's hold on Tabitha had begun to fade. She had known it would piss Tyler off to see her speak to that man. The man seemed unkeen to have a conversation – he noticed Tyler's gnarled face glaze over – and before a full conversation could start Tyler strode through the room and dragged Tabitha away.

Outside, centred in their shared vacuum of rage, they were unaware of the crowd that gathered to watch. Tyler had a bottle of lager in his hand that he stabbed at the air causing beer to spit from the neck as he shouted and gestured. Steam rose from his hot sweaty shoulders in the frozen late-autumn night. Tyler and Tabitha were inches from one another's faces when he called her a slag. The word left his mouth in a cloud of condensation and appeared to hover for a moment between them. She took a step back and without a thought her fist tore through the insult. There was no skill or plan to the punch, she just punched blind, and when the mist cleared Tyler held his nose as blood dripped through his fingers. A great cheer rose and she saw a blackness pass over Tyler. He turned and smashed the bottle he still held against the low wall that surrounded the building. His eyes grew wide and empty and his mouth turned up at the edges. As he lunged for Tabitha two men sprang forwards and grabbed him by both arms. A scuffle broke out as another tried to prise the glass from his hand. Tabitha didn't wait to find out the results. She ran from the shouts, applause, and approaching sirens.

She still wandered alone when the cold dawn approached, the numb houses and streets motionless, moonless, and foggy. If she went back to the flat Tyler would be there waiting to slice her throat. She couldn't go back to her mum's after the argument they had about Tyler. Her mum had said he was no good but at the time Tabitha thought her mum would have said this even if she had brought home Prince William. She couldn't go back there drunk, banging on the door in the dark, makeup-stained tears down her cheeks.

She found herself outside that house. It was old and the architecture enhanced its façade unlike the brick box where she lived. It was a large house that exuded a privileged peaceful aura. That privilege sneered at her and gripped her inside as the saints in the stained-glass of the porch windows smirked. Who has church windows in a porch, she thought as she picked up a rock from the edge of the garden. Who can afford a stained-glass porch when people are on the streets, she justified as she hurled the first at the faces that gazed down despite not giving a shit about people on the streets. It missed so she picked up another. This one hit but bounced off so she found a bigger rock and hurled it with all her strength. It punched through with a high-pitched tinkle and left strips of jagged lead in its wake. She looked for more and threw and continued to throw as upstairs someone turned on a light. When every panel was broken she sat down on the sharp confetti and waited for the police to arrive.

A wind blew and rain tapped on the window which changed to a drum of hailstones within seconds. The thick overcast sky made the room gloomier but Marguerite didn't turn on a light. With her teacup and saucer cradled neatly on her lap she gazed through the weather out at the back garden.

'So why did you break my windows?' said Marguerite. Tabitha told her the truth.

'They looked smug,' Tabitha said with a shrug. It was the truth. Tabatha thought she saw a trace of a smile on Marguerite's lips.

'They're allowed to be smug,' she said after a moment of thought, 'they're saints.'

When the police arrived Tabitha was calm. A female officer approached her with a pair of handcuffs while her male colleague remained next to the car. There was a constrained tension as if they were prepared to face a tiger and had found a stray moggy. The woman spoke to Tabitha in a gentle voice as she came near, perhaps wary that the cat might be vicious anyway. Tabitha wasn't and, as the handcuffs clicked around her wrists, the atmosphere exhaled. She was put in the backseat and taken to the police station. There she was processed and her mum, as her only next of kin, was called to fetch Tabitha in the morning.

When she arrived back at her childhood home, she took a deep breath and, contrary to what she'd expected, felt a gentle warmth in her body. They didn't say a word to one another. Tabitha's mum went straight to the cluttered kitchen where BBC Radio 4 played, as it always had even if no one was in there to listen. Tabitha walked past the front room, where the saggy battered blue sofa still sat in front of the television, and up the stairs to her bedroom. She closed the door behind her. The room still caught the morning sun as she remembered. Gold and mellow. When she moved into the small flat with Tyler she had to leave a lot of her things behind and had assumed her mum would have chucked a lot of it out but she hadn't. The shelves were filled with dusty books from her school days and things she'd collected like a smooth marbled stone from a beach on the Gower and a green-silk pincushion edged with tiny Chinese acrobats. Tabitha took off her heels. Her ankles were bruised from where her feet had rolled over as she'd walked the streets drunk. She took off her clothes and left them in a pile on the floor and then rummaged through the musty white-slatted-doored closet for pyjamas. She found some that still fitted. They'd been a birthday present from her aunty when pink and ponies had felt too childish so they had never been worn. She put them on. The brushed cotton was warm and comfortable against her skin which ached all over from the hangover that started to creep through her body. She closed the curtains and got into bed. She slept until the sun had gone down.

Tabitha had expected a row but it didn't happen. When she got downstairs her mum was sitting in front of the television with a blanket over her lap.

'There's soup on the cooker top if you're hungry,' she said. 'I bought some of the crusty bread you like.'

She looked tired, but it had gone eight. Tabitha went into the kitchen and helped herself. She then sat with her mum on the sofa and ate while they watched a TV programme where people watched TV programmes. Afterwards they went to bed with very few words spoken. Despite the lack of communication it didn't feel the same as the familiar joint silent treatments that had happened in the run up to Tabitha moving out. Back then, even though they wouldn't speak a word to one another, the atmosphere was split and fragmented as if they were screaming at one another. This quiet was different. Tabitha had passed the crisis point of a fever and now it had broken she'd begun to recover. She lay with boils lanced, as black bile drained from her body, and engorged leeches fell off.

They finished their tea and Marguerite took Tabitha out to the back garden.

'This is what you can do for me,' she said, pointing up. The hailstones had subsided to a fine mist-like drizzle. Through the rain rose a garden on a steep incline. The centre was an untidy lawn which was bordered on either side with overgrown sweeping flower beds dotted with leggy shrubs. At the top of the hill stood an old stone wall that was about the height of a two-storey house. Brambles and honeysuckle clawed through the masonry and hung down as a green curtain. From behind this curtain emerged the spires of Llandaff Cathedral, which dwarfed Marguerite's home and grounds. It wasn't until the two women moved through the wet grass, halfway up the slope, that Tabitha got a real sense of the size of the garden.

'You won't need any gardening knowledge,' Marguerite said to Tabitha, 'it's gone from garden to overgrown disgrace.' She paused for a moment to catch her breath before she strode on. Tabitha felt she knew more about disgraces than gardens.

When Marguerite had first moved into the house the garden had been much worse than its current state. It was Marguerite who had cleared the brambles and the rubbish as she planned and shaped to a detailed picture in her mind. Originally she looked into having the slope terraced but that would've required an expert and the prices were too high. Instead she worked all summer to reduce the visual impact of the gradient with clever planting and the lines of her newly dug borders. She became fitter than ever before. At her peak Marguerite could mow the entire lawn in under thirty minutes. The mower she used was petrol and, due to the placement of the lawn, she chose to stick with the heavier durable type even when lighter electric mowers became available. The day she found out newer models had levers to make the rear wheels move she rushed out to the garden centre to buy one. When she got to the shop, she walked around the shiny and colourful new technology for an hour but came home empty-handed. As she browsed, she concluded that if machines took over all the difficult jobs in life the human body would become soft and weak. They'd also take away the sense of accomplishment she'd always valued. She remembered the same discomfort when she'd gone from doing laundry by hand to using a washing-machine. The washing-machine cut the time spent housekeeping by more than half but she always treated it with suspicion. As the new mowers of her neighbours needed servicing more and more and eventually broke, hers kept going. There was less on it to go wrong, she would tell them. As middle age turned to old age and her neighbour's physical frames became bent and fragile and led to frequent trips to the doctors and increasing stays in hospital, her body remained robust and strong. When Marguerite was asked how she kept so healthy she would regale them with the story of the trip she took to the garden centre more than twenty-five years before. Her neighbours would smile and agree but behind their compliant nods they would put her health down to good genes rather than a bulky lawnmower.

Even with the help of her reliant and hefty machine she now approached ninety and the scramble to get to the upper borders was too much. The mower had simply become too heavy for her to push. She mowed the lawn for the last time when she was eighty-eight. She got halfway through and reached the top of the slope when she turned and the mower pulled from her grip. Instead of letting it roll to the bottom she tried to catch it and as she lunged forwards lost balance. She ended up tangled together with the mower in the bottom hedge, her leg covered in petrol that had leaked from the upside-down engine. Marguerite drove herself to A&E to get a gash on her knee seen to as it was a little deeper than the ones she would ordinarily sort herself. The doctor was astonished at her story and insisted she get an X-ray to check she hadn't broken anything. She assured him that she hadn't and that she wasn't in any real pain. The X-ray came back clear but the doctor told Marguerite that at her age she should not do such heavy work. He told her that she should get a man in to do it. Marguerite thanked him politely and went home to complete the job she'd started. As she cut the rest of the grass she felt a change. The slope looked steeper than before and each time she reached the top her heart began to thump in her chest. After she'd finished she put her loyal mower back in the shed and clicked the padlock shut.

Marguerite had tried several companies, some broader odd-job handymen, some garden maintenance, and some specific lawn care, but she felt embarrassed by their vans outside her house. Her elderly neighbours had either moved to homes or had died and she was now surrounded by younger families and couples. When they saw Marguerite was hiring help for her garden, they assumed the worst and began to drop by regularly to check on her and ask in condescending tones if she needed anything and whether she was well. Eventually she decided not to hire men to do her garden and wouldn't always answer the door when people came round to check on her.

Tabitha's legs ached as her feet slipped on the wet grass and she strained to follow Marguerite. It was a while since she'd done any physical activity, apart from a fight in the street every now and again.

'Are you sure you can't do this yourself?' Tabitha muttered through gasps, her cheeks red with effort. Marguerite continued to point out the plants and shrubs that peeked through the weeds as she rattled off a list of common names mixed with occasional Latin. A magpie lifted into the air from the long grass. Its loud chatting echoed off the tall cathedral boundary. The bird gripped to a branch of a tall leafless tree next to the towering wall and continued to swear at them. When they reached the top Marguerite was quiet. She bent over to pull out a weed and her weight began to topple forwards but she righted herself before she fell. The garden sighed with Marguerite and she began to make her way back down towards the house. Tabitha glanced about her as she followed and her mouth screwed up before she asked, 'when should I start?'

Back in front of the house Marguerite showed Tabitha the shed. She unlocked the large, rusted padlock with a key she had in her skirt pocket. Iron-infused rainwater poured from the barrel of the lock as she took it from the latch. Inside the shed was a strong smell of solvents and paints. The shelves were crammed full of old metal boxes, tins, and bottles. The lawnmower was in the middle of the floor, and attached to the walls were hooks that held gardening tools. Marguerite informed Tabitha that other than the mower she kept no power tools instead preferring the natural peace of the garden to be undisturbed. Tabitha rolled her eyes at this sentiment as she had hoped she'd have the chance to use a chainsaw.

'But even if I had a chainsaw,' said Marguerite, as if she could see Tabitha's thoughts in the air, 'you wouldn't be allowed to use it.'

Two

Tabitha knocked at the door – two weak taps – and it opened in an instant. She swayed – eyes wide with shock – and regained her balance while she attempted to form normal sentences at a regular volume.

'I'm here,' she slurred and after a pause she blurted, 'to fucking work!'

Marguerite was silent as she led a wobbly Tabitha through the hallway and into the front room. Once manoeuvred before the couch, Tabitha wilted into the seat and exhaled heavily through her nose.

'Well you're certainly dressed for the occasion,' Marguerite said as she gestured to the spiked high heels and bodycon dress that had rolled up her thighs to show her knickers. Tabitha gave a snort of laughter and giggled as she closed her eyes. She heard Marguerite's slippers on the carpet scoot into the distance.

Tabitha's mum was working nights. She worked in supported accommodation for vulnerable adults. Some residents needed care twenty-four hours a day and seven days a week so the staff would rotate their shifts. She'd often do a week of shifts that ran from nine in the evening until eight-thirty in the morning. Tabitha had wanted to behave but by ten o'clock everything on the television was either a gameshow or a talent show, both aimed at an audience with sludge for brains. She tried to be that audience, but she couldn't identify or empathise with the contestants. The participants' personal stories were forced and even if the heart of the tales were sad the very fact they were used to make "good TV" cheapened the tragedy. It was clear to Tabitha that the "mean" or "cynical" judges were staged so that the audience felt delighted and warm when the judge's "heart of stone" was softened. After a couple of glasses of her mum's white wine Tabitha began to heckle, and by the time she had finished the bottle she was in her going-out clothes as she switched off the box.

The kitchen table had always been a point of communication between Tabitha and her mother before Tabitha had moved out. Because of her mum's shift work a note was often required but finding pen and paper, especially in a hurry, could be difficult. Instead they scratched notes like runes to one another in the tabletop with a small knife or even a fork if it was first to hand. There was an archive of messages that dated back years. The main theme of Tabitha's notes was that she was going out with friends and that she would be back at some indistinct time. Tonight was no different as she scrawled, 'Out with Chantelle – back by morning,' with the point of the corkscrew she'd used to open the wine. As Tabitha left and locked the front door she assured herself that it would only be for a few drinks. In the morning she had to go to that posh old bat's house and walk up and down her mountainous garden.

A washy pleasant cloud already surrounded her when she met Chantelle in the city centre. They found a table and Tabitha told Chantelle a redacted version of her recent adventures. Chantelle didn't hear about the extent of Tyler's violence as Tabitha thought this would put a downer on the night. Also, because Tabitha didn't want to put herself in a bad light, she omitted the age and vulnerability of Marguerite. While they caught up they drank. After each drink she bought, Tabitha would say, 'this is the last one.' This continued until around the sixth or seventh glass when Tabitha's priorities changed. The important thing now was the man with the smirk of a smile who had approached her at the bar and asked if she was French and if she was menstruating. Tabitha snorted and said that she hadn't heard that one before. He was well-built, dark-haired, and energetic with an unusual name which she didn't catch; she thought it had sounded foreign but she couldn't detect an accent. He wasn't her usual type. He had a band T-shirt on with some illegible spiky name and tattoos of skulls and demonic-looking shit. She generally went for the clean-shirted and shoed type with a lot of cologne but this guy seemed more interesting. He asked if she would like a drink and, as one of her rules was never turn down a free drink, she accepted. It wasn't until the bar called last orders that Tabitha realised she'd lost Chantelle. She lazily looked round the immediate area but figured her friend must have found a man or else got bored and gone home.

Tabitha woke up early. She'd been dreaming but couldn't remember the details. She was short of breath as though her chest was constricted. At first she thought he'd fallen asleep on her but he was over the other side of the bed. It was possible she'd drifted off for just an hour or so as they only reached his house a little before dawn after leaving a club at four in the morning. She remembered flailing her arms wildly to something loud, fast, and heavy that didn't have a tune or intelligible words. She didn't remember much of what happened when they got back to his except his advances had felt like something between sex and wrestling. He was strong and rough as if he'd been starved of physical contact for some time. This made her suspicious as he wasn't unattractive. A recent news report was brought to her mind. A young woman had a one night stand with a man who'd just been released from prison. The young woman met her end when he stabbed her to death shortly before another resident of the halfway house walked in to find the man chewing off her face. The building Tabitha was in didn't seem like a halfway house and the man seemed too well dressed to be a cannibal: although the bloke in *Silence of the Lambs* was smart. She pushed it to the back of her mind. The sex wasn't unpleasant, though something of a shock at first. Afterwards she felt exhausted and battered to a certain extent. Something had changed in him now though, almost as if he was a different person. Through the blur and shimmer of her drunkenness the darkness in the room was dense and through it the walls of the bedroom looked like bare stone, dusty and veiled in cobwebs. She thought of the halfway house of horrors again and put on her clothes quickly before she tiptoed out the door. She was about to click it closed when she thought she heard a voice say, 'good luck.' She stumbled down the stairs as fast as she could muster and onto the pavement outside which she didn't recognise. After some wandering she found a street she thought she knew. It worked out she was closer to

Marguerite's than she was to her own home. So without any chance to sober up she staggered to her first day of gardening.

Her skull felt as if it had been split in two. She opened her eyes a fraction. They felt gluey and sore. It took her a few moments to work out where she was: the flat, home, Chantelle's, the stranger's house, or, least likely but most accurate, Marguerite's. She tried to move but groaned instead. Over her bare legs was a floral quilted bedspread and on the little table next to her sat a glass of water and two tablets. As usual the front room was dim but while she was in this state the gloom felt comforting. She slid onto her side and took some deep breaths until a wave of nausea had passed. A voice through the shadows caused her to jump.

'How are we feeling?' Marguerite had been motionless in her armchair on the other side of the room. 'A little tired and emotional today it would seem.'

Tabitha nodded, unable to think of a suitable excuse. The only way Tabitha could label the conversation that followed was blackmail. It soon became obvious that Marguerite knew the system better than Tabitha would have liked. Tabitha could only assume that in Marguerite's previous meetings with the police she'd probed for every iota of information about Tabitha's background and the Criminal Behaviour Order. Amongst other things, Marguerite was aware of the exact parameters of Tabitha's CBO and that Tabitha had broken those conditions by being out all night drinking. She also knew how close Tabitha was to fucking up her entire life. That she was one step from prison and subsequently on track to a future where people wouldn't trust or employ her. Today was the crux of her existence, Marguerite had told her, the fork in the road where one path led to Tabitha alone and dying in a piss-filled alleyway and the other to a life she wanted. Tabitha muttered that it was all a bit melodramatic but she realised that Marguerite did have her by the balls. In her delicate state she gagged at the thought of owning her own set of testicles and squeezed her forehead until the wave of nausea and the heart that beat in her brain had stopped. All this aggression for a bit of gardening that she would have done anyway. Maybe she wouldn't have done it to the highest of standards, but she would have helped the old bitch out a bit. Though it was now apparent to her that the old bitch didn't want to be helped out just "a bit".

When Marguerite began to set homework, Tabitha knew that more would be required of her than a tidy garden. By now she'd worked at Marguerite's house for two weeks. Although the social workers had set a manageable twelve hours over three days, Marguerite had her working close to full-time. As Tabitha worked, Marguerite would sit on a white plastic patio chair and watch. She'd made Tabitha pull the patio chair out of a skip outside the house on the opposite side of the road. A man had come out of the house and asked her what she was doing. Tabitha looked for backup to where Marguerite had been standing on the pavement but she was gone. After an awkward conversation there was a clear sense of distrust from the neighbour. He kept his eyes on Tabitha as she crossed over the road with the filthy chair and waited for Marguerite to open the door. Her cheeks became hotter and redder the longer it took and by the time she got back in the house she was furious. Marguerite laughed until her throat became hoarse.

Tabitha started with the lawn. She felt uncomfortable filling the mower with petrol, as if it would blow up in her face for some reason. The smell of the fuel lingered in her nose for a while which convinced her that if it did blow up the fireball would enter her nostrils and ignite her head. After two lengths of the lawn the thought of her head igniting was a comforting prospect. The mower was heavy and the slope even steeper than it had seemed when they had walked it the week before. As Tabitha pushed, her feet slipped, and the mower rolled backwards towards her. If she couldn't push anymore the machine would crash into her and cause swollen colourful bruises on her arms and legs. The only chance she had for a rest was when she got to the bottom of the hill again. On top of the weight of the machine the grass had also become too long for the mower to cut in one go. This meant that Tabitha would have to do the whole lawn three times, starting with a higher cut and decreasing the height of the blades each time until it was finished to the standard that Marguerite desired. Unfortunately the highest setting wasn't enough to get through the thick thatch of lawn, which meant that grass jammed the blades which in turn stopped the engine. Each time the blades jammed Tabitha flinched at the shriek from the mower. She would then have to tip it onto its side and manually pull the sludgy green clog from the workings. After the first day she'd not even made it past halfway on the highest setting. She went home covered in scrapes, scratches, and bruises, with stains up to her elbows. She went to bed early and had a full night of deep sleep superimposed with photographic images of grass.

The next day Tabitha woke with an ache in her legs, but as she began the first ascent of the lawn, she found her feet adjust beneath her as if her body had learnt something new without her knowledge. She cut the rest of the lawn on the highest setting and half on the next height down before it was time to leave. She went home that night with a small sense of achievement and maybe a little excited. The day after brought more pain than anything else. Her body had become exhausted and the work felt even harder than it had on the first day. Marguerite only allowed her two breaks in the day: a short tea break in the morning and a half an hour at twelve-thirty where Marguerite gave her a sandwich and a banana. If Tabitha stopped outside of these times Marguerite would tell her that the grass would grow back before she had even finished the lawn once and would remind her, in one way or another, of the life she had waiting for her in prison. By the end of the week Tabitha's body was beyond the initial ache and instead felt as if half of her blood had been drained from her limbs. Clusters of weakness gathered in her shoulders, chest, and hips and made her lose interest in everything but sleep.

After Tabitha had cut the lawn and had finished the first two weeks, Marguerite gave her the Friday off, but only so that she could use the extra day to study. Marguerite handed Tabitha a book about lawns and lawncare and told her that she would be tested on its contents on Monday. Tabitha was also given a copy of the King James Bible, of which she was to read the first chapter. Tabitha wasn't religious and had not been brought up in a religious household. This felt like a cheap attempt to recruit her into the church. She studied the book on lawns as best she could over the three days but left the Bible unopened.

After the initial cut the lawn became easier to run over with the mower. Tabitha could finish it in one day, as long as she did it once a week to keep the length down. After a month she had built a routine that she would mow every Monday, whatever the weather. Her calves and thighs soon became stronger, and she could feel her abdominals working hard to stabilise her core as she strode up and down the slope. On the other days, under the watchful eye of Marguerite, she began to clear the large borders that'd been overrun by brambles, nettles, and grass. The thorns broke through the thin gardening gloves Marguerite had given her and stuck into her fingers. They also grabbed at her arms and wrapped themselves around her ankles as if they were sentient and fought for their lives. A stream of swearing followed these attacks which in turn was tailed by Marguerite's chuckle. The roots of the brambles had formed large bulbus knots over the years that clung deep in the soil and required Tabitha to dig around them. As she dug, the rest of the bramble whipped about and caught in her hair and scalp until Marguerite had had her fun and suggested a pair of secateurs or loppers to cut them off at the base first. For a while it made the task easier until the wooden handle of the spade, which had become rotten in the shed, snapped and Tabitha was left with a stump that she had to bend right over to use and exert extra force to lever out the bramble crowns.

The brambles were not the only difficulty. There were also tree saplings that had grown too big to dig out easily, expanses of underground nets attached to stinging-nettles, and huge carrot-rooted dock leaves that seemed to push straight to the centre of the earth. Each evening she went home tattered, bruised, and scratched. Her arms and back ached from tugging and pulling and, when she closed her eyes, she had visions of leaves and brambles as clear as if they were still in front of her. Despite the complaints she slept better than she ever had in her life and each morning she woke up and got on with it again. She could see her progress as she moved through the borders: clumps of mature perennials revealed as tips of new growth that peeked from the soil, the shrubs as they flexed and spread their branches after their restrictive weed cages were removed, and bare dark earth ready to receive new plants.

Despite the obvious improvement, Marguerite still watched and set Tabitha homework to do on her days off. Tabitha was given books on flowers, pruning, wildlife, horticultural Latin, and vegetable gardening, even though Marguerite had no vegetable beds. Marguerite still set Tabitha sections of the Bible to study, which inevitably led to an argument when Tabitha hadn't read them, and sometimes threats from Marguerite that involved the original blackmail. But Tabitha was satisfied now that Marguerite wouldn't tell her social worker about the mistake. As long as she continued to do a decent job on the garden she knew Marguerite wouldn't want to lose a good thing. Despite this the clashes still enraged Tabitha.

It was after one of these arguments, on a Monday morning, that Tabitha stormed out into the back to start her weekly mow. It had rained for several days without much relief and there was drizzle in the air as she pulled at the starter cord. It didn't start straightaway and she pulled again with the anger of the confrontation tense in her neck and arms. It started and she strode away up the slope, her feet turned out to the side to help her grip the wet grass. It was on her way back down that she slipped and let go of the mower. She and the machine landed in a heap at the bottom of the lawn and she screamed in frustration and pain at her now bruised shin. Marguerite loomed over her. She told Tabitha to get up and Tabitha told her to fuck off.

'This is your fault, you old bitch,' she said, 'you have to make everything harder than it has to be. You just want to see me suffer.'

'The only person who makes you suffer,' Marguerite replied, 'is you. Now get up.' Marguerite pushed her with her foot and repeated for her to get up.

'Fuck off,' Tabitha said again before she started to cry. They were tears of anger but she didn't know why she was angry or where to direct it.

'You can't always blame something else, and you can't always expect someone to pick you up,' Marguerite said with calm authority, and then 'get up.'

As the weather warmed more presumed lost perennials and bulbs wove their way through the soil and brightened the edges of the garden. The deciduous trees and shrubs burst into leaf in what seemed like a day while birdsong and the hum of insects threw the patch of land into life. It was a Friday afternoon at the beginning of July when Tabitha found that there wasn't really anything to do. Sure, there were little weeds and the odd leaf to pick up – there was always something to do – but the big work was finished. Marguerite must have noticed this too because when Tabitha turned she was standing at the bottom of the slope with a jug of lemonade, two glasses, and a plate of biscuits on a tray. They spent the rest of the afternoon in the sunshine on recliners as they talked about the garden; the things Tabitha had learnt, the plants that had come into their own, and ideas to improve for the future. It had got to five o'clock when Marguerite finished her third glass of lemonade and said, 'that will be my last.' They said their goodbyes as usual but this time Marguerite stretched out a hand for Tabitha to shake. She thanked Tabitha for the work she had done and told her that being able to see the garden back to the way she had planned made her very happy. It was a warmth that Tabitha hadn't seen in her for all the months she'd worked at the house.

When Tabitha got home that evening she felt comfortable. The muscles in her shoulders felt soft and relaxed. When her mum came home Tabitha smiled at her and asked her how her day had gone. As she lay in bed that night she picked up the copy of the bible that Marguerite had given her and began to read. In the beginning, her eyes began to feel heavy after only a few sentences; the language was strange and rhythmic. She read up to the part where God planted a garden eastward in Eden when her eyes started to close. She opened them again and reread the sentence before they closed again. This happened a few times until she fell asleep and the bible dropped from her hand and onto the floor. Tabitha's mum turned off the light an hour later when she went to bed.

Three

It should have been obvious to her that the set-up was there. The finished garden, the last lemonade, the thankyous, the handshake – but when was real life like that? When did you get to say goodbye? On Monday the weather wasn't extraordinary in any way. It was a comfortable temperature with sunshine that peeked through the clouds every now and then. When Tabitha arrived at the house she saw the front door open and men walking in and out with bits of furniture. She frowned but was distracted by thoughts of the garden, thrilled at the prospect that more flowers might've opened over the weekend. She didn't stop to question until she was in the centre of the front room and saw the sofa, which she had passed-out on at the start of the year, being removed by two scruffy men who didn't acknowledge her presence. As she felt a sudden shift in normality a younger man in a suit came out of the kitchen and looked at her.

'Can I help you?' he said.

'Where's Marguerite?' she said. When she got to the 'M' in 'Marguerite' she'd already figured it out.

The young man turned out to be the family solicitor. He let Tabitha stay after he learnt her name matched the name in a note Marguerite had left by a stack of books on the kitchen table. Tabitha put them in a battered carrier bag and went into the garden. She sat with caution on one of the loungers, fearful that it might vanish beneath her. She placed the books on the floor. The bag flopped to the side and allowed the books to slide out one by one with light thuds as they each hit the patio slabs. Tabitha left them where they fell and sat for more than two hours as she stared at the borders and listened to the birds quarrelling in the hedges. The garden didn't look as good as she thought it had on Friday. There were still plants wrapped up in weeds, the lawn was bare and yellow in places, and the flowers that had opened were raggedy from slugs and snails.

Her mind was blank as the time passed. After a while the solicitor came out and told her she needed to leave. He told her the only known family Marguerite had was a cousin in Austria and that he could give Tabitha their contact details if needs be. She shook her head. This appeared to be an attempt at warmth towards Tabitha but his lack of empathy made the exchange uncomfortable. Tabitha gathered up the books and left without thanking him.

Tabitha didn't tell her mum that the old lady had died. She felt no real sadness to speak of, only a sense that she'd begun to watch a film and the electricity had gone off in the middle. The books remained in the bag on the floor of her bedroom. She didn't need to learn anything more about gardening and there was no one to push her into religion. Her body still felt sore from the work she had done for Marguerite so she decided to write off several days for recovery like an elite athlete after a big competition. She spent her time sleeping late and watching daytime TV. Her mum noticed Tabitha wasn't working and with care, asked why. Tabitha told her the old lady had died so she couldn't do the work anymore. When Tabitha had spent a week slumped in front of antique and light detective programmes, doubt began to creep in. She had time to worry that she hadn't completed the hours of work assigned. She fidgeted and grumbled to herself about this until she could take no more and decided to ring the social worker to tell her what had happened. After a few phone calls to and fro it was decided that due to the unusual circumstances Tabitha was free to get on with her life as usual, provided she still adhered to the original conditions of her CBO.

Tabitha checked the obituaries each day in her mum's newspaper, convinced she'd done this before Marguerite had died and on the Friday after she'd found the vultures clearing Marguerite's house, Tabitha happened to chance upon the date of the funeral. The obituary was simple: Marguerite T Martin, 89, of Llandaff, Cardiff, passed away at home on the 14th July. Funeral to take place in St Mary's Church in St. Fagans this Friday. Tabitha had been to St. Fagans when she was a child. It seemed to be a necessity that every child in South Wales would visit the museum at least three or four times throughout their school life. It wasn't a usual museum where the class would file through a room to glance at dusty artefacts behind glass, reading the text beneath them for the first few before interest waned and the children began to chat and annoy the teacher. St Fagans was outside like a village. The numerous and varied buildings had been moved brick by brick from other locations in Wales and rebuilt on huge estate grounds to make an historical jumble. Outside each construction was a sign that explained the basic facts of where it had come from, who had owned it, and what it had been used for. Inside the buildings hung the gloom of history and ashy fireplace smells. There would also be a member of museum staff cloistered away in each, ready to answer questions. She wondered how bored and lonely the museum staff got on a quiet day, cloistered in each of these buildings, alone in the past. The effect of walking through the eras one after another wasn't that of time travel – even when viewing the row of terraced houses whose décor changed through the decades – but of time being non-linear, deposited in chunks through space.

Tabitha had thought that the museum was actually St. Fagans and had no idea that there was a village with a church. On Friday she made her way to the funeral. She'd never been to a funeral before. She'd not really known anyone who had died before apart from a boy who was her age at school. He'd killed himself and his two friends in a car accident a couple of years after they had finished their GCSEs. She'd been told by her friend who'd seen it in the local newspaper. 'What a prick,' he'd said, 'killing your friends just because you want to show off.' The boy had taken the corner while going three times over the speed limit and ploughed into a tree on the opposite side of the road. He'd also nearly killed a mother with her three-year-old in an oncoming car. Tabitha couldn't remember speaking to the boy once through school. His mum must've felt bad when she got the call.

When Tabitha was small, her mum had cut ties with her parents and the extended family after a messy divorce from Tabitha's dad. The devout Catholic family had been outraged at the idea, whatever the reason, and were unable to fathom their daughter's motives. So Tabitha had not got to know any elderly relatives. She was spared news of their ailments, hospitals trips, and deaths. She had also avoided a religious upbringing. She could count on the fingers of one hand the times she'd been into a church. Most visits had been with her primary school choir, not a real choir but a group of children singing for their parents, around Christmastime to sing carols. She'd also gone on one religious studies trip to Gloucester Cathedral, where they sat in on a service. The huge ornate cavern of the nave had shrunk Tabitha as she walked through the studded wooden door. As they took the tour she touched the prone figures on the tombs of noblemen, bishops, and kings. King Edward II had the hands of two small angels as his pillow, their faces raised to the sky in exaltation or maybe from the strain of keeping Edward's heavy stone head aloft. The tombs were smooth and cold. A million hands polished carved edges. The class, including Tabitha, messed about, ignored the teachers, and sulked about how boring it all was.

Dressed in her longest black dress, that was too short for a funeral, and a navy cardigan she'd borrowed from her mum to cover her arms and chest, she stood outside the church gate, not wanting to go in. She watched a few people filter in and after a while decided to follow a small group that turned up. She walked up the path behind them, three adults and a child, but before they reached the door they veered off into the graveyard and gathered around a headstone. She paused and wondered if anyone would notice or think it strange if she left. It was likely they would, so she held her breath and entered.

Inside, the church was much lighter than Tabitha had anticipated. She'd thought the stained glass would dim the sunshine but instead it was softened and warmed. A woman at the entrance passed Tabitha a small booklet of hymns and prayers with a sympathetic downward smile. There was no photo of Marguerite on the front, only her name, her year of birth, and year of death. Past the pews sat the coffin, closed and still. Tabitha half expected the lid to be open with a queue of people waiting to file past the corpse and kiss her cheeks as they said their tearful goodbyes. It always seemed this way on the TV though maybe they were American. Instead, there was a scatter of attendees seated throughout the church in quiet thought with hands rested on laps as if at a bus stop. No one wailed at the loss or questioned the death's authenticity.

It seemed that most of those in attendance knew Marguerite from the church and Llandaff Cathedral. There was no family to stand at the front and give a detailed and moving eulogy. The vicar had only known Marguerite in her later years when she had begun to visit St. Mary's every Sunday morning. Although the vicar attempted to give the funeral a personal feel she was limited and the service felt sparse. Tabitha wouldn't have noticed either way. Between prayers and bible passages the older women warbled along to the organ as it played Jerusalem and The Lord is My Shepherd. Tabitha held the booklet up in front of her face at these points in case someone saw that she hadn't joined in and asked her to explain herself.

As they walked from the church the vicar shook the hands of each person. Tabitha tried to slip by without being noticed but the vicar caught her eye and held out a hand. Tabitha shook it without looking up and started to walk away but her hand wasn't released.

'Are you a family member?' said the vicar. She'd probably recognised everyone else at the funeral.

'No,' Tabitha muttered as she tried to walk off.

'Do you know any of her family?' she continued, 'we're concerned that they might not have been made aware of her death. Marguerite paid for her own funeral.'

'I just did a bit of gardening for Marguerite. That's all,' she said and went to leave again before she saw the genuine concern on the Vicar's face. 'Look ... all I know is that a family member in Europe paid to have the house cleared when I went over there last.' Tabitha's voice cracked. She looked at her feet and felt a hand on her shoulder.

'Will you be at the burial?' the vicar asked, her voice now gentle. Tabitha shook her head and walked off with more force this time.

There were no plans in place for a post-funeral reception, but

Tabitha wouldn't have gone even if there had been. When she walked out of St Mary's Church grounds she saw the big green gates of the back entrance of the museum. Visible through the curled wrought iron was a wide straight drive that led to the Elizabethan manor house and manicured gardens. A large cloud passed across the sky but a light breeze blew it on and the sun emerged and cast pleasant, dappled light through the leaves of the trees that lined the road. Tabitha turned right and walked to the pub that was a few hundred feet up the road and there she spent the rest of the afternoon drinking.

What followed was a trip into the city centre and a binge that surpassed even her pre-CBO drinking sessions. She wandered from pub to club to pub making friends and enemies and taking phone numbers of people she'd forget by the morning. By the time midnight had come and gone she started to attract the attention of the bouncers and quite soon she was denied entry everywhere she tried. Frustrated, she went into a corner shop and bought a bottle of Jack Daniels. She swayed as she flicked through her purse at the counter. Back on the street she sat with a homeless woman and drank until she offended her by attempts to destabilise the woman's religious beliefs. It seemed inconceivable to Tabitha that even at rock bottom, with a life that had played out like a Greek tragedy, a person could defend an absent God. The homeless woman accepted this was Tabitha's opinion but when Tabitha suggested that the woman's hope and faith in God kept her on the street the woman got up and walked off without saying a word. Tabitha watched her leave and drank more.

Somehow Tabitha managed to get home, because the next thing she was aware of was her bedroom ceiling, tangled up in her duvet covers with an empty whisky bottle. She was still in her black funeral dress and, with the least movement she could muster, slipped out of it and fell asleep again.

When she woke up the next time she had to move because her bladder was bursting. Every part of her body hurt and as she raised her head it swam, spun, and then throbbed with skull-crushing pain. She made it to the bathroom but had to throw up before she peed.

Afterwards she threw up again but it was mostly dry and she felt like a spider's husk. She staggered back towards the bedroom. There was a mirror on the wall of the landing, and as she passed by, she caught a glimpse of herself. She stopped and looked closer. There was a huge black bruise around her left eye and a cut on her nose. A memory came back, fragmented but clear enough. She staggered off alone after the homeless woman had walked away. As she stumbled along the pedestrianised city centre she saw him – Tyler. Tabitha didn't know whether to engage or try to move past without him noticing. He was with a group of friends. They were as drunk as she was and they shouted, pushed one another, and threatened members of the public as they moved through the street. She remembered how her heart had thumped in her chest as he got closer and felt a mixture of excitement and fear. The feelings she had when they first met surfaced and betrayed her and there was no way she would have passed by without the group spotting her anyway. She was a young, incredibly drunk woman showing a lot of leg and Tyler had homed onto that before he even knew it was Tabitha. When he was close enough to see her face through the drunken mist the catcalls turned to anger. The rest was a blur but she thought the other men had pulled him away as she lay on the floor and that might've saved her. There was big, raised marks on her legs that looked like she'd been kicked. One had the printed pattern of the sole of a shoe.

Tabitha's mum had a day off and brought water to her in bed and cups of tea and soup. She didn't mention that Tabitha had been drinking despite this being obvious. Instead, she acted as though Tabitha had a genuine illness like a bad tummy. She took care of Tabitha as her little girl again. When she looked at the bruises on Tabitha's face, Tabitha thought she saw tears in her mum's eyes. By early evening Tabitha began to feel better and made her way downstairs to sit with her mum in front of the TV. Tabitha's mum made hotdogs and they ate them and watched a silly show where people had to run an obstacle course without falling into the pools of water below. After the hotdogs they drank cold cloudy apple juice which made Tabitha's mouth feel fresher and she fell asleep with her head on her mum's lap.

The next day Tabitha found it difficult to get out of bed. There was no reason for her to get out of bed but even the things she liked to do, like watching TV or having a bath, felt a bit pointless. When she thought about getting up, she would drift off to sleep again. She didn't leave her room that day and when her mum came home from work Tabitha told her that she wasn't hungry. This went on through the following day but by the third day her mum insisted she ate something. She went downstairs to eat and afterwards went to sleep in the armchair. Her mum woke her with a soft nudge and told her it was bedtime. Tabitha nodded but stayed up a while. She went into the back garden and sat on the dirty patio furniture. There was a large full moon that made everything look pale. Grasshoppers chirped in the tangled grass that edged the lawn. Tabitha's mum never gardened and the back hadn't changed since they first rented the house following her parents' divorce. The only thing Tabitha's mum did was spray weedkiller onto the patio and leave the brown withered weeds there to be replaced over time by new ones. It was a balmy night, the kind that might hold an epiphany of some sort. Tabitha waited to receive it but nothing came. She was bored. Bored of sitting on the patio, of the progression of life, and of being Tabitha.

She went back up to her room and sat on her bed. She felt like a child on the naughty step without any clear understanding of why she was there. Maybe someone's god was punishing her. Though from what she understood gods were more into corporal and capital punishment rather than supernanny techniques. A frustration rose in her which she relieved by kicking the bag of books on the floor. She didn't get a great connection with her foot and instead of hurtling into the wall, as she hoped, they toppled from the top of the bag like dominoes. Thud, thud, thud. Guilt replaced her frustration and a wave of sadness drained her body while she tried to stack them back together. Through the fog she saw some of what she expected, a few Christian books mixed in with gardening books. There were also some she couldn't place. She initially thought they might've been Christian novels by their names: *The Book of the Law, The Lesser Key of Solomon the King*,

The Greater Key of Solomon the King. But then there was *The Book of Lies* and *Magick Without Tears.* Amongst the books was also what appeared to be a document. On the front it said *St Fagan – A Hagiography* and underneath someone had written in red pen 'A Pseudohistory of the origins of Christianity in Britain'. She was unsure of the word hagiography but she could guess what pseudohistory meant. She flicked through the document and found the main body of text that had been heavily annotated. Some were typed in footnotes, and some added on top in the same handwriting that was on the cover. It seemed likely this had been done by Marguerite.

I

Noviomagus

It was amidst a thick broth we first spied Britannia. Her cliffs and bays formless and incomplete through the haze. As we docked at Noviomagus I prayed in private. I then gathered my modest bundle of things and joined my travelling companions on deck.

I had journeyed from southern Gaul to the very edge at Morini before I met the men whom the Pope himself had sent to Britannia at the request of King Lucius. When first we met names were exchanged and Deruvian asked if I was a Gaul, to which I replied, 'certainly not.' Deruvian gave a grunt and we moved on. The two men made no attempt to address me afterwards and spoke little to one another. I assumed they were tired from the road.

I was to accompany Fagan and Deruvian in part as a translator and in part as a handmaid of sorts. When we reached the ships in Portius Itius we would have to negotiate our passage to Britannia with the captain of a merchant ship. Portius Itius[7] was an odd place. There were crumbled inns dotted about where men languished. They also sat stone drunk in the dirty streets. It was late August and although the weather was mild, the sky was overcast and plants wilted as if through boredom.

We waited several days for a ship to arrive and when it did the captain was entirely unhappy with allowing a woman on board. By this point it was already clear that neither of the services I had to offer would be needed. Fagan took the captain aside. Fagan was a large man who stood a hair's breadth too close for comfort when he wanted something

---

7. The place names appear correct when checked against genuine Roman documents. If this had indeed been written by a woman of the 12th century, she must have been a remarkable woman even without the psychic powers she claims. Few women (and in fact most men) at this time were not educated and literacy was kept for a select few. Though there is a chance the stories may have been passed on orally, the details may not have been accurate.

from you. He appeared to guide a person to his line of thought with naught but a thin scatter of words and a few subtle movements. Even in silence he kept the souls of those around him on their knees. Not once did I see a man challenge him. Rarely would you see a person ever pause to study his countenance. At first, I presumed this to be heavenly spirit that filled his body. After all, Angels are so often required to implore their observers to not fear them.

As you can imagine, it was not long before we were allowed to board the merchant ship. We were on our way to Britannia. Once on this ship I wandered what use Fagan and Deruvian would have for me. I felt certain that if Fagan had no use for me he would not have persuaded the captain to let me board and I would have been left in Gaul.[8] I watched the shore as the boat pulled away from Portius Itius. Its hull creaked against the quiet flow of the channel and my scalp puckered beneath my hair. The men on the boat called to one another, muffled through a veil of wet fog.

The mist hugged the boat tightly throughout the journey. The captain had remarked on the calmness of the currents. Calm water usually pleases sailors but as I moved across the deck the men on board each seemed occupied in their own minds. They stared into the haze at childhood memories, loved ones, the horrors, the cogs of the universe.

Eventually I settled for a spot on the portside and watched the sea ooze past. The damp worked into my clothes and flesh as my view blurred to white. I saw Ezekiel's valley of dry bones made soggy, moss-coated ribcages, and empty skulls filled with tiny pools, microcosms of squiggly larvae. I spoke to the bones, but they did not stir. The last dregs of cartilage were chewed away by insects in front of me. As I gazed on, a dark forest rose around, the patter of rain dripped from branches and hit the muddy mushroomed ground. I heard a footfall squelch behind and as I turned, I saw Fagan, his hair dewed. When I looked in his eyes, I saw the depth of the forest disappear into them.

---

8.   It is most unlikely that a woman would be included in a mission such as this though for the sake of artistic licence and a good story the character seems an entirely useful device.

30

He spoke, words reverberating off droplets. 'You'll be expected to go in with us.'

I was catapulted back on deck. My mouth opened and shut like a fish until a few words seeped out and I managed to ask, 'where?'

My mind floundered between vision and reality, Fagan lifted me and leapt overboard. He answered in one word, 'castle'.

Fagan's voice had a strange intonation. He had an accent, but it was impossible to locate. It was nomadic as it wandered from place to place, expression to expression. I tried to protest, indicating that I was entirely unfit to enter the castle of a king, but I spoke to the back of his head as he turned and moved away into the veil.

After I was sure he had gone, I went below deck to find a more solitary place to spend the rest of the journey. I found a quiet corner of the cargo hold and tried to dry off by wrapping a blanket around my shoulders. I propped myself up against a sack of grain and slipped in and out of sleep with the movement and groans of the ship. Because the air was so still the rest of the trip took four hours.

I was awoken by muted shouts as we moved towards Noviomagus. That indistinct shore caused a squall in my chest, but my mouth moved to smile and with teeth bared I reached Britannia. Beside me Fagan's blank face stared ahead. Deruvian saw my teeth and smiled an impish smile. He put his hand on my shoulder but it sank beneath his touch.

Noviomagus was like a carcass alive with maggots. A smell of rot greeted us as we alighted and after only a few feet I was caked in mud. It was busy and louder than I had expected. I'd heard no one cared to enter Britannia unless absolutely necessary. The Romans referred to Britannia as the 'Dark Island' and Pope Eleutherius had described it as godless. The natives still held huge parts of the country despite repeated attempts to conquer their land. There were deep forests that had not been entered or charted due to the disappearances of many who went in them. If Fagan and Deruvian had heard these stories they had not made a great impression.

We walked through the backstreets of Noviomagus. The ground was thick with human shit. In time we came to an inn where Fagan said we would stay for the night. Fagan must have seen the displeasure creased on my nose because, before we went in, he mentioned that the place was reputable. Deruvian gave a pig-like snort at this comment. Inside was what I expected. The straw on the floor was encrusted with vomit and the room was filled with men at every level of drunkenness. A few turned to look as we entered but snapped their glances back to their ale when they saw Fagan and Deruvian.

Fagan went off to find the inn keeper and left me alone with Deruvian. He took a chair out and motioned towards it. I sat down and placed my hands in my lap. They felt awkward and treacherous as if they would somehow betray me. Deruvian asked if he could get me a drink. There was a smirk in the corner of his mouth. I declined. My reply was sharper than intended and, ashamed, I looked down at the tabletop. It was carved with all manner of names and symbols. I heard him laugh as he began to walk away. 'Wait,' I said. He stopped to hear a reason for my outburst. The blood quickened around my body as two men on the table next to me turned to look. One had an eye missing and, instead of a patch, the cavern of his socket was left exposed. The other man smelt of piss. I saw Fagan's soundless form move back into the room. 'Never mind,' I said as Fagan rejoined us. Deruvian shrugged and walked off to get a flagon. Fagan beckoned to me in silence. His eyes would not quite meet mine.

I woke early on my first morning in Britannia. As pale light eased into the eastern sky, I knelt by the window for more than an hour and prayed. Afterwards my knees were bruised, and my hands were cramped into claws from the cold. Outside a gentle rain had begun to fall. I took in a deep breath and the sound of the drops on the roof alleviated the tension in my shoulders and as they dropped, the back of my neck relaxed and clicked. A thud on the door reversed this. 'Come,' said Deruvian's voice through the heavy wood, 'we have a long way to go.'[9]

---

9. As works of fiction go, so far, it has a reasonable start. We have an interesting character set up, a young woman who is obviously religious, two improbable holy men. There has been some sense of overshadowing of danger and violence and to add to that a wisp of sexual undertone. Really all you need in a good yarn.

Four

Apart from the young Marguerite's peppy footnotes, Tabitha found the writing difficult to get through and she'd drifted off a couple of times before she made it to "All you need in a good yarn". She forced herself to read to the end of the chapter before she put the open chapter on the floor and turned off the bedside lamp. She lay awake for a short time. She saw the ship in the darkness above her head and the outline of a man begin to form. Her eyelids closed and she heard Marguerite mutter that Tabitha had one last piece of homework to complete.

Tabitha woke up around seven o'clock, which was early for her. The sun shone into the back of the curtains. A thin strip escaped through the middle and cut across Tabitha as she lay beneath the duvet. She felt well rested, better than she had for some time, and she stretched as the remnant of a dream faded away. She was used to odd or scary dreams but this one felt different. It was more like a memory, where she was in bed in her own room. There was a weight that kept her pinned to the mattress and a tightness in her chest. All around her stood silver trees and the air was cool and fresh. She'd sensed the heaviness that held her down wanted to frighten her so she raised her eyebrows, pursed her lips, and sighed through her annoyance. After a battle of insolence the pressure left.

Later that morning her social worker came to call. The social worker was past middle age and was round. She had a dumpy body and large face with circular glasses that sat on her flat nose. A few long wiry hairs grew from her chin. As she bustled in she seemed surprised to see Tabitha with a smile on her face as she folded laundry. Tabitha's mother whose shift didn't start until the afternoon, was also stunned and suspicious of this change. She kept this to herself but an occasional side glance towards Tabitha gave her away. The social worker was keen to get Tabitha back on her feet and asked how Tabitha felt about more garden work. Tabitha said she would be happy with this and the social worker alluded to a job that might be available.

By that Sunday the job had been secured. It was only two days a week and she would share the work with a professional who worked the other days. She would assist in the maintenance of the grounds around Llandaff Cathedral and help out in the garden of a vicar who worked at the Cathedral. There was the chance to improve the borders dependant on available funds for new plants. Her wages would come from the vicar's discretionary fund. The social worker made certain to add that the vicar could choose to give this to anyone he thought needed it most. He'd met Marguerite when she accosted him outside the heavy cathedral door. She had been persuasive. According to the social worker, Marguerite had insisted he follow her to her house and see what Tabitha had done with her garden. Marguerite had described and hammed-up Tabitha's difficulties with a school that had given up on her and a boyfriend who had beaten her and led her to a life of substance abuse. It seemed Marguerite had not detailed Tabitha's crimes and the vicar had been touched by the story. Marguerite had given him the number of Tabitha's social worker and he soon rang and told her how impressed he had been at the resilience of a young woman in such difficult circumstances. He was also overwhelmed by the determination with which she helped Marguerite and sad that Tabitha had now lost her mentor. Marguerite had painted Tabitha as a repentant Magdalene. This made her feel like a fraud as she took the bus ride from her house the following Monday.

Her first day followed a weekend of heavy thundery downpours. The rain softened overnight and dawn pushed the clouds east. Despite the hour, the humidity was high and clung on her forehead and under her arms as she walked to the bus stop. The road was quiet as she waited. It was less busy through the summer without the school traffic and today was muffled further by the heavy air. Canopy steam rose into the air from the warmed branches of a wooded hill which rose up behind houses that were so sharp they looked as though they had been erected yesterday. The mist soothed their edges like a security blanket. A robin hopped over the pavement and fluttered onto the bench next to Tabitha. He looked at her with a sideways head, his tiny eyelids visible as they flashed over black shiny beads. With closed lips and a still heart she watched and wondered if she should feel moved by this perfect creature in miniature. He seemed to posture with an affected charm that boasted his existence to her. As the bus hissed and came into view, the robin, shamed by his arrogant display, flickered off into a nearby shrub. The wheels came to a stop and the doors sighed open. Tabitha boarded and threw her change in the machine at the front. The driver kept his gaze ahead and once she'd taken her seat the vehicle groaned into movement. She caught a glimpse of the bird as they pulled off. He hopped from one thorny stick to another with his beak open as he tried to sing above the noise.

The vicar was old and slight with cottony tufts of white hair that slid down the side of his head and filled his ears. Reverend Geraint Edwards was a kind man, though he shoe-horned biblical stories, quotes, and sentiment into most conversations regardless of topic. He had come out of the vicarage to meet Tabitha as she disembarked near the Cathedral. As she approached he held out a hand. His handshake was soft – a soft grip with the velvety tissue-thin skin of someone who'd not done a day of manual work in his life. The vicarage was a large five-bedroomed house, built in pale natural stone with medieval arched windows and doors. The Reverend Geraint had not married so had no family to fill the vicarages he'd moved into over the course of his vocation. Instead he filled them with possessions – rooms stuffed floor to ceiling with books, papers, and knick-knacks and souvenirs from every place he'd visited through the Church or personal travel. Tabitha followed him through small corridors of space between masses of junk. As she sat on a chintz armchair she was cocooned by cushions. The vicar had a plate of biscuits and a pot of tea waiting and he poured her a cup and offered her sugar and milk.

He talked for over an hour about the parish, the parishioners, and the church. He told her about coffee mornings and evensong and fundraisers for spires, organs, the poor. She tried to listen with apparent intent, now and again she opened her eyes wide and rubbed them to stay focussed, but she didn't know the people or jargon so could only watch as the words floated in the air between them and disappeared. The vicar darted from one path to another, his guest left further and further behind until she could only spot a glimpse of the crown of his head as it bobbed off into the distance. It was a while before she caught up with him and realised he'd begun to talk about the work that was required in the garden. He was in the middle of a list of jobs. The grass in the graveyard would need to be cut on a regular basis. The lawnmower should not be set any lower than three because the ground was mossy and the blades would turf it up and make a horrible mess. There were two large flower beds on the way into the Cathedral that were in dire need of attention. They were filled with groups of perennials that would probably need to be split when the autumn came and shrubs which had started to turn leggy and unsightly. The weeds had begun to take over and some of the plants had already been lost to them. There was also space for at least one other flower bed to be created but a plan would have to be put to the management team of the church. Tabitha could choose which two days she would prefer to work on, though Sunday would be best avoided for obvious reasons. Tabitha wasn't sure how obvious the reason was but she had an idea that churches tended to do more stuff on a Sunday. Her hours would be from nine in the morning to four in the afternoon with a courtesy break for lunch in the middle. After this was explained, Reverend Geraint took the teacups and the teapot into the kitchen on a tray. He then shuffled out the front door with Tabitha in tow so he could show her the things he'd already described to her in great detail.

The graveyard was an old one and the soil, encompassed by a wall, sat high above the ground level outside and was pushed into lumps and waves like a choppy green sea. The headstones stuck up like crooked teeth, some so ancient that their words had been weathered to a whisper of an indent. Other graves were marked by huge Victorian monuments – weeping women who leant exhausted on urns, broken columns, and detailed wreaths. Amongst these shone the odd glint of dark marble from a few modern additions.

The empty plots were reserved for only the eldest and most devout members of the Parish and one or two for children whose tragic deaths had shaken the community, though the vicar explained that due to the amount of people interred over the centuries the empty plots were never really empty.

The vicar showed Tabitha the borders and then inside the Cathedral. The studded wooden door was down a large set of stone steps and once through, there were more steps. The descent weighed on Tabitha's shoulders and chest and she felt her body shorten as she stood beside the pews to gaze at the ornate chasm above. The saints in the stained-glass windows looked down on her, their superior mouths downturned to pious judgement, and pinned to a large arched concrete structure in the centre of the nave, a huge statue of Jesus looked up a touch to avoid eye contact.

There was a mix of old and new, concrete and stone, tombs and flowers. To the left of the nave was a room dedicated to men in the Royal Welch Regiment who had died across many wars. There was a big leather-bound book with names and dates, the most recent being the previous year. During the tour a constant stream of facts, stories, and biblical quotes and passages flowed from Reverend Geraint but as he and Tabitha reached the altar he fell silent and stopped. He then asked the question she had anticipated would come and was unsure how to answer.

'Do you attend church, Tabitha?'

'No, not really,' she muttered and cleared her throat as she waited for an answer or a retraction of the job offer. Neither came, the vicar just gave a solemn nod and continued. After he'd finished his tour, the vicar took Tabitha back into the vicarage for more tea and biscuits before he sent her home 'for a good rest' in order to start the proper work in the morning.

She ate tea with her mum that evening and went upstairs. The document Marguerite had given her had flittered in and out of her mind throughout the day. When she read the crumpled pages she hadn't really considered the content or what it meant, but as she trailed behind Reverend Geraint that day, and got lost in his facts, her thoughts had occupied themselves. It was strange that a person who wished to forge an ancient document to change history would add an outlandish foreword that credited the whole thing to some mad Spanish occultist. There was also something about the guy who travelled with Fagan that seemed familiar. She had given Deruvian a face and that face – like the *Jesus in Majesty* at Llandaff Cathedral – refused to look at her.

II
Via Romana[10]

The mist had not lifted. Although the road was straight, I could see no further in front of me than the head of my horse and the arse of Fagan's. Before we left Noviomagus, Fagan had gone to a stable and left with three of their best horses. He did not say how much he had paid for them, but I assume it was much lower than it should have been. In hindsight I realise he might not have paid for them at all.

Through the blanket the sound of hooves clacked loud on the stone. Apart from this and an occasional deep cough from Deruvian, we travelled in silence. No birds sang and the rain continued, gentle but persistent. Within half an hour the water had soaked through much of my clothes, and I shivered. An animal fur was thrown over me from Deruvian's pack. I did not lift my chin to look, just thanked him quietly. We continued at a reasonable pace. After about two hours I could hear a stream to our right as it bubbled alongside. Its watery giggle as it swaggered over rocks joined with the music of the rain. With nothing in front to see, I stared down at the road; the stones, smooth from wear, fitted together with precision. I saw a vision of men, bare-backed and dewed, as they dug huge lengths and depths of foundations. Their well-developed shoulders and backs ripple and then cripple beneath time. A myriad of knees worn raw as they grovel to hammer down the surface.[11]

---

10. A little unimaginative in the titling.
11. The details here are quite specific for the alleged age of the document. Did the Medium have possession of an older text? Though some classics were studied by the Middle Ages, which was key in developing Europe, it's unlikely someone such as Gueraula de Codines would have access to them. These details didn't jump out at me on the first readthrough but now they seem an obvious anachronism. It's possible this is a faked historical document, maybe from the Edwardian times when mystery and the Occult was popular. A similar example would be *The Black Pullet*, though this was conveniently anonymous. Finding the original document could remedy this.

The cracks between were filled with a cement of sweat, blood, and dirt. Their lives a small price for order and convenience of travel. I looked back, now aware that my horse had walked past the other two. They stood still and looked ahead. Fagan grunted to Deruvian about natives and Deruvian, without concern, asked if we should be concerned. When I followed their gaze I recoiled in horror. My reaction caused the horse to skitter and back away. Its eyes were wide as it tossed its head from side to side. I leant over and soothed the creature though my heart tried to climb from my chest.

A solitary archway stood astride the road. It had crumbled without maintenance but remained ornate. A rope had been slung over the top and attached to the end was a human being. It seemed to be a woman, but it was difficult to tell. The body had been peeled like an orange and the chest cracked open and emptied. A snake's nest of entrails had been pulled from the abdomen and hung to the knees. The rain had washed the body structures and made them shiny and clean as if a human was meant to look this way.[12] Bright iridescent tendons and rich purple and red muscles. She then came to me. She stood in front of me, naked down to her insides, and spoke. 'I burn . . .' she said, 'I burn and it won't stop.' I felt her scrubbed muscles as if they were my own. 'Beware of false prophets,' she said with a gurgle, blood caught in her throat, 'inwardly they are ravening wolves.' She pointed at Fagan and Deruvian, their outlines smudged through the shroud of my vision. She then vanished, and the men came back into focus. Fagan muttered that it was a warning of some kind, 'but not for us.' I gasped and his head snapped up to look at me. I shook my head as my breathing slowed. Fagan kept my gaze for a moment, something he had not yet done. It was a peek into a deep well, an attempt to see the bottom which you know must be there. There was no doubt a stream ran through but there was no way to prove it and the only way to know if it was poisoned would be to lower a bucket and take a drink. A risk I refused to take.

---

12. This seems very graphic, even in terms of gothic horror of the 18th and 19th centuries this seems out of place. The Edwardian occultists may have been shocked by this (Mr Crowley aside) which makes the initial disclaimer seem more necessary.

Deruvian suggested we press on as long as we were not in any immediate danger. I agreed, the sooner we could get to the king the sooner we could wash and have a bed in which to sleep.

We continued. Deruvian and Fagan seemed no worse for the scene we had encountered. My horse was still spooked. She threw her head from time to time and clattered her hooves when we came across a fox. The road opened out as the stream that had travelled alongside us joined to a river. A vast marshland lay on either side. Great reeds rose up and a heron took flight and disappeared into the whiteness. I could hear the croaks of frogs grate amongst the boggy moss, and the plops as they jumped from pool to pool. Lunch time had come and gone, and my stomach gurgled with the sounds around us. Deruvian must have heard because he rummaged in his bag on the back of his horse and pulled out a loaf. He tore it, put half in his bag and gave the other half to me. Our fingers brushed as he passed the food from his hand to mine. I thought about the poor woman we had seen, her body like a butchered lamb, hinged open and exposed to the world. My stomach growled again. Deruvian stroked his hand with a smile on his lips before he retook his reins.

I chewed as the horses pressed on, and after I'd finished, I still felt hungry. I closed the gap between my horse and Deruvian's, and glanced up at him, but his face remained forwards. After the third or fourth glance he explained that we needed to be frugal as we did not know exactly how long the initial journey would take. I was a scolded dog as it begged at a dinner table. Though I wanted to tell him I did not need more food, my stomach gave me away. This was the first time that I understood the journey would not be a simple Baptism before we returned home. It had become apparent that the full reason for our visit had been kept from me and might well remain so as I followed like a blind woman.

The day had begun to end. We could not see the sunset through the mist, but the paleness had darkened to a grubby yellow-grey. The frogs grew louder as the sky turned murkier. Before long we reached the edge of a forest and followed the road in for about half a mile. Fagan stopped his horse and dismounted. He suggested that to go any further would make little sense and that we might as well make camp there until morning. I dismounted and went to find a place to piss[13] as the men erected a leather sheet to sleep beneath. As I squatted in the undergrowth, I heard a voice: *They are ravening wolves,* it said, *ravening ... beware.* Through the trees a rabbit squeal was followed by a great cheer from Deruvian. By the time I returned he had skinned it and taken out its insides. Fagan finished hanging the leather sheet as I assisted Deruvian in making a fire. We managed to light it despite the dampness that soaked into everything, including our bones. I shivered as the flames licked at the dark and started to warm me. I had not noticed how damp and cold I had become until it came into contrast with the heat of the fire.

With vegetables from the supply bag, the rabbit Deruvian had caught, and a cooking pot, I made a stew for our small party. Deruvian sat near the fire with me, but Fagan lay on his back at the side of the camp. Now and again I would squint through the night at Fagan until Deruvian whispered with a smile that Fagan was listening. He listened for threats to us, Deruvian explained, and to check that we would be safe sleeping there. I nodded and stared into the centre of the burning sticks. My mind drifted and I murmured, mostly to myself, that the scariest thing in the forest may have been Fagan himself. Deruvian laughed and gave me a pat on the back, which knocked my face close to the blaze. I could feel heat rush to my cheeks, not from heat but from embarrassment.[14]

---

13.   An odd choice of word from the translator, if indeed it has been translated.

14.   There's an odd gap that follows this paragraph – as if something had been missed out. Though why they would keep the gap I do not know. Possibly it is a formatting problem. I did make a start at trying to track down the original text and am surprised to say that I already have a lead. At first I inquired by telephone at the Louvre who suggested it might be more useful to contact the British Library in London. According to their records it had been requested there for study. I managed to speak to the Head Curator who was certain they had had such a document at one time but thought it had returned to Paris, though instead of back to the Louvre it might have been sent to the Bibliotheque Nationale de France. I went into the Bibliotheque but the Curator was off with a bad back. I made an appointment to see him the following week, leaving details of the document so as to give him a chance to find it before my visit.

I had made this journey as a pilgrimage. I had hoped to feel closer to God, but with each step across those satanic lands I felt myself move further away. That night after we had eaten and the two men had put their heads down, I prayed. I prayed for guidance, I prayed for my soul, I prayed for safety from the savage natives, and for anything else I could think to pray. For a moment I watched the faces of the men in the light of the dying embers. Deruvian's lips curled at the edges, something of a smirk remained even as he slept. Fagan's brow ruffled down towards the bridge of his nose. He looked more strained in sleep than he did when awake. We cannot control our minds as we sleep, we cannot control the worlds there and the spirits who visit us. Fagan was a man who contorted the waking world to his whim. I felt an urge to pray for some fortification against Fagan but feared it might be blasphemous. Fagan came recommended from Pope Eleutherius himself. He could not be a false prophet or a wolf.

III

Bodunni[15]

The depths of those forests were darker than I could have imagined. The morning split red across the sky as we loaded up the horses. When we moved on, a stag crashed through the undergrowth and stood in our path. It was motionless for a moment, eyes white, rolled back in its head, foamed mouth, body steamed with sweat and heat. In that pause it seemed to gauge the threat we posed comparative to what had it on the run. Its head twitched in the direction of Fagan before it darted back the way it had come. The fog had cleared, only a mist remained, and it rose into the sky from the top of the tree canopy. There was a deep succulence to the vegetation and a bogginess to the ground. Moisture dripped in great beads from the foliage onto the ivy that choked the forest floor. A drop hit me on the crown of my head. My heart raced. The rustles and scuttles in the undergrowth, the sudden bird calls of fear, the shadows in the distance had me on edge.

Emperor Hadrian had records made and crowed like a cock about his hold on the people of Britannia. Though it was no secret he spent his time being scrubbed, oiled, massaged and engaged in debauch, sexual acts with young men in *Aquae Solis*.[16] Hadrian surrounded himself with sycophants who ensured everything in his world was to his liking. As far as he was concerned, he held complete control over the conquered nation. When he asked if a wall would keep the Caledonians out, his men would say, 'absolutely, yes,' and build it for

---

15. This might be a slip of tongue that could help to rule out the possibility of this being a collection of stories passed on orally to the medieval author. The word *Bodunni* is thought to be a mistake by *Dio Cassius* who wrote accounts of these tribes at the time. The actual tribe was known as the Dobunni and it seems odd that this mistake would be duplicated unless the writings of *Dio Cassius* had been studied.

16. Again, this seems rather graphic and gratuitous in all but the most modern of literature.

him right across the breadth of the country. Whatever Hadrian believed, Britannia was not domesticated yet. The revolts had not ended with Boudica and the Iceni. There remained isolated pockets of resistance in hard-to-reach parts of the island. These were guarded by bloodthirsty natives that lived outside of Roman rule and Roman law. They refused to bow to the Emperor or Jupiter and gained notoriety across Britannia and beyond for their crimes against nature and against God. I had even heard about them amongst the civilised people in southern Gaul. As long as Hadrian stayed in his baths, his soldiers would have no motivation to enter the backwoods and risk their lives to put out these fires.

The trees had moved from leafed to needled. Nothing grew beneath their dry spidered branches. Their scent was bright and shadows as dark as holes in the veil between this world and the next. I peered into the gloom beneath the trees that lined the track. Every so often I thought I could see structures in the distance, built beneath the canopy, shapes obscure and geometric. After some time even the rustling of the creatures had stopped. It was a still day and no wind brushed through the forest. The horses provided the only break in the silence, their hooves, the odd toss of a mane or quiet whinny. I tried to talk to Deruvian, asked him why we had not stuck to the road, but he did not seem comfortable to talk. He turned his head a fraction to tell me it was quicker. His eyes remained on Fagan all the while.

I yawned, my eyelids grew heavy and although I tried to stay focussed my thoughts took the reins and trotted into abstraction. There was a man with an axe and he hit the back of it against a tree in a drip-drip rhythm.[17] The blade faced out and with each blunt blow hit him in the shoulder, large chunks of flesh removed as it went. The man had a blissful smile on his face despite his ever-growing wound. He turned, looked directly at me, and frowned.

---

17   These odd little asides set a scene though it seems doubtful someone recalling a story would remember such details… However, I think it is worth reminding myself here that I am not trying to prove nor disprove the existence of the paranormal through the soothsayer but rather get to the bottom of whether this document is a more modern construct of the macabre Victorian/Edwardian occultists.

An arrow whistled through the air and hit him in the forehead with a wet thud. My horse screamed and I was thrown from his back. I awoke in time to feel my head hit the ground hard.

Deruvian was standing over me. Through a haze I could see his wide-wild pupils, his mouth upturned at the edges, his fists sticky with blood. He shouted something I could not make out; it was in a language I did not recognise. He ran from my view and an arrow thumped into the ground where he had been. I rolled away and scrambled to get up. My chest heaved as I tried to catch my breath. I caught a glimpse of Deruvian as he bounded off into the trees. I could not see Fagan. As things fell into focus all that remained were the men's horses, frozen to the spot as they tossed their heads. My horse lay on the ground, froth around its face as it gasped in air. The arrow had hit it in the neck and blood sprayed from the wound in a dramatic arch that had saturated my shoes and the hem of my shawl. After several agonised minutes it let out a strangled wheeze and died. The other horses moved further away and nibbled at the grass on the edge of the path. I squinted into the dark beneath the trees. I held my breath to listen. There was silence. No sound of the men returning. I began to wonder what I should do if they did not return, if they were dead somewhere. Should I look for them? Should I continue to King Lucius or return to Gaul? I sat next to the horse's body and waited, the only thing I could do that was within my power. Something told me that Deruvian and Fagan were alive and they would be back. As the woods grew darker, my stomach growled, and a dog howled its response in the distance. Deruvian and Fagan's horses stirred at the sound and I looked up. A few metres away stood a figure, head covered by a large hood that cast a shadow over the face. They took the reins of the horses and a female voice said, 'follow.' I remained still as she walked, leading the horses away. She stopped and turned; 'Follow or die.' I followed. I heard a movement from behind and turned to see a small group of people surround the horse's carcass. They started to chop at its leg joints and neck with big blades.

We walked through the undergrowth. I felt sick, and my head throbbed, maybe from the knock I took to it when I came off my horse. I had to pause to throw up a few times, my guide did not stop to assist me. At times I had to listen for the rustle of her steps and follow the noise alone. I began to smell smoke, and soon after we reached a large clearing where I could make out around twenty or so roundhouses, black against the backdrop of the forest. The women who gathered amongst them turned to stare as we arrived. A young girl ran up and took the horses from my guide. My guide muttered something to her in their native tongue and we continued to the biggest roundhouse. Inside a fire burned and lit three faces. They were all women. Beside the fire lay two huge dogs, or what I thought were dogs. As we moved closer, I saw they were wolves. I could smell the mucky dampness in their coats and a strong whiff of carnivorous breath as one opened its mouth to pant. 'Sit,' said one of the women sitting towards the back, her eyes fixed onto mine through the gloom. They reflected the flames like torches at a distance. I sat down on a fur blanket and shook from the core of my being. The tremor came from the injury to my head rather than fear. The fire and a chance to sit outweighed any anxiety I had. Another woman handed me a cup of water and I drank it in one only to feel my stomach turn again. I held the vomit down but at this point my vision started to blur and my head drooped forward, chin on chest. The woman on the far side of the room spoke again, asked in broken Latin why we travelled through their territory. There was no aggression in what she said, more like genuine interest. I tried to make a sentence but acid from my stomach began to rise again and I threw up. At once, one of the wolves hauled itself to its feet and mooched over to lick it from the dusty dirt-floor. The other two women in the hut went to my aid and the one who had spoken rose to her feet as the roundhouse vanished. We were amongst the leaves of a spring forest. Sunlight dappled fairy grass and birds sang on every bough. She was young, a child really. The two wolves joined her side, and she knelt beside one and drank from its teats. On the little finger of her left hand was a claw instead of a fingernail.[18] The forest sank away into the ground, and she

18. There are many legends that involve children raised by wolves not least Romulus and Remus and the founding of Rome. It seems highly probable that similar myths would have existed in Wales which has a rich history of folklore. It is difficult to find text of these as many of these tales were passed on orally.

stood atop a hummock, lifted her head to the sky, and screamed, not one of pain but one of war. She and the two wolves then attacked an elephant. Although the giant beast dwarfed their forms, it was no match for their ferocity. They tore open its stomach and were drenched in gallons of blood and insides. This attack continued for hours, until the sun set and darkness fell over my entire being.

I awoke to the sound of Deruvian laughing. I had been laid on top of a low bed in the same roundhouse. Light shone through the door and hit the back wall, bringing some light into the room. A form, black in front of the sunny door, ducked in. Deruvian's smirk came into focus. I said, 'so they didn't kill you.' My voice cracked, throat sore from vomiting. He told me to get up as we needed to get back on the road. We were behind schedule. Another person hurried in, it was the woman from the night before. She began to question me, a stream of questions in dog Latin, 'You're Tavia, aren't you? You're from Gaul. What's it like in Gaul?' As I tried to answer she would not wait to hear them, she would interrupt my pauses with, 'Yes, go on,' and 'it's ... ?' and 'What? What is it?' I had to run the words together in order to form a sentence before she began to talk again. An assault of further questions would then follow. 'Why did you come to Britannia?' 'Do you like it here?' She spoke over me, even before she had digested the previous words. This was the way conversations would go with Ciwa. It was as though she had rehearsed them beforehand and would use the rehearsed lines whatever the response. Deruvian told me, through the interrogation, that Ciwa was head of the village and, with raised eyebrow, the strongest warrior in Britannia. 'Do you eat the same as we do? I really like to eat deer and rabbit. Do you like deer and rabbit?' she said as a woman entered with a pot of stew. Ciwa filled a bowl for me and as she passed it over informed me that it had been made from my dead horse. The woman who had brought the food gasped and chastised her like a mother correcting her child. She explained to Ciwa that I might be upset because I had ridden the horse all the way here, and that we had probably become friends. There was a pause before Ciwa burst into a fit of giggles at the thought of a horse as a friend. She told them that Tavia would not make friends with horses but stared at me as she said this, as if in need of confirmation. As I opened my mouth to reply, Deruvian chirped in, 'she would not have a horse as a friend or anyone for that matter.' He winked at Ciwa which caused her to giggle again.

Fagan waited for us at the edge of the village. Ciwa had donated a horse to me, it was stronger and more responsive than the one that had become a stew. Fagan looked straight ahead and started off on the road again.[19]

---

19. Again this passage appears quite modern. There's a familiarity of style that's not present in the formal writing of the 14th Century. I could've put this down to the translator's artistic licence but the situation has changed. I went to the Bibliotheque Nationale de France and saw the original document. It is without doubt the genuine article. The Head Curator was still off but one of the young interns took some initiative and found the work for me. With cotton gloves I was allowed to study the text and accompanying notes that had proved their authenticity by the relatively new science of carbon dating. The work had all been handwritten in Latin though not in the way a calligrapher of the time would do so. My Latin is rusty but, from what I read, my copy is close to the original. The intern was as surprised as I was that such a rare and apparently important document seemed to be all but forgotten in their vaults. I saw the additional pages that bore text in the Enochian alphabet and glanced over several maps of Britannia and ambiguous diagrams before the Library had to be closed. I made an appointment with the intern to come back the following morning.

On arrival the following morning I found the Head Curator had returned. I told him that I had an appointment and he told me that I didn't. I asked about the intern, and he said that he didn't work there anymore. I asked him about the document, and he said that it did not exist. I tried to show him the notes I had, and the copy of the translation but he ignored me. After about fifteen minutes of this charade he began to get angry and told me to leave. When I didn't, he called the police so I left. As I left, he screamed after me that I was banned from the Library and that he would put a description of me behind the desk so the other staff would know. He said if I tried anything else he would have me arrested. I went back to my apartment and cried. At this point I wasn't upset about the document but shell-shocked at the confrontation. Now as I write this, I realise the significance of this interaction. It is quite possible that I should've never seen the document at all. It seems it would be in the Church's interest to keep it under wraps. Although it's doubtful it actually documents the rise of Christianity in Britain, even pseudohistory can be a powerful thing. Take Geoffrey of Monmouth and the tales of King Arthur, for example, these were taken as fact for centuries until more recent study disproved them and even then when people hear a story they like they are reluctant to let it go. It seems the University was also aware of the dangers this document could pose. I might've done more harm than good by seeking out the original. Now they know people are aware of its existence, it will be buried even deeper into the archives, if not removed entirely and destroyed. I suspect that the carbon dating had been an attempt to disprove its age. A document traced back to the Edwardians would have had much less historical weight than something from the 14th century. I have no real proof now that any of this has happened or that I have seen the original document, but I feel honour bound to continue with this project now. To assess the rest of the work with its age in mind and to try to get something published so the world can decide for itself.

Five

Tabitha thought she saw him the next day through the window of the bus, behind the reflection of her own face shaken into double vision. Last night she'd read more than she intended and was tired. Maybe she'd begun to drift off to the whirr of the engine. It was probable that her one night stand was around the area, as she'd walked from his to Marguerite's, but for him to spot her through the bus window and to give her a sullen raised hand seemed less likely. She turned her head after they passed but saw no one on the pavement. The woman sitting next to her gave a concerned sideways glance as Tabitha's inhales became difficult and her heart thumped loudly enough to be audible. The woman moved to another seat as soon as one became available.

The rest of the day passed as normal and when the late afternoon sun grazed her nose, she'd mowed the lawns and begun to clear one of the borders. The sky had been clear and a breeze kept the day fresh. When it was time to go home Tabitha felt restored, as if a tangle of thought had started to unwind itself. At his request, Tabitha made her way to the vicarage to collect that day's wages from Reverend Geraint. Until the church could set up formal pay with an external company this was how she would receive her money. Tabitha thanked him and declined an offer of tea with the excuse that she needed to get back to hang washing outside for her mother. She headed off to find a pub.

She walked into The Nag's Head and glanced around to check no one she'd met from the Cathedral was inside. Though her CBO had come to an end she preferred to keep her reputation as a reformed Magdalene that had secured her the job. The Nag's Head was a friendly pub with places to sit inside and out. The building was old with dark oak-panelled walls. The restaurant had been updated to give the feel of a modern bistro; however much of the regular clientele still perched on stools in the bar area and played darts at the back. A television was on the wall and though it was generally used for the rugby, today the BBC news channel was on. Breaking stories chased each other's tails at the bottom of the screen and the presenters updated – but in most repeated – the same things over again. As Tabitha waited her turn at the bar there was a report on an American missionary who had travelled by river boat to an isolated tribe in South America to bring them Christianity. He didn't succeed in converting them to a life of religion. As soon as his foot hit the bank he was shot full of arrows. The tribe took his body and left it near a logging company's on-site headquarters. There he was picked at by the rainforest until they found him in the morning. No one really seemed to be watching the television. She asked for a pint of cider.

Tabitha took a seat outside on a picnic table. Other than two men around her age sitting a few tables away, the rest of the patio area was empty. They were not like the men she saw in the pubs she had frequented in the past. They had piles of books around them and were wearing checked shirts and tweed. The larger of the two was smoking a pipe but rather than being an affectation, their nercy demeanour suggested this eccentricity may have been genuine to their class and lifestyle. When she heard mention of Jesus, Tabitha remembered Marguerite had told her that young people came to Llandaff to study and train to become ordained as members of the clergy. The smaller man's voice reached her ears as a low mumble and blurred with the sound of traffic on a nearby road. The man with the pipe, who seemed the stronger character, responded to the sound in his own clear stage voice. He explained that the role of Mary Magdalene in Christ's story may be a more prominent one than they were led to believe.

'Well, I think we're in agreement that it is highly likely that the original text was edited at some point in its two thousand years on Earth,' he said. The other man cleared his throat and moved as if he wanted to speak but was interrupted. 'Come on, Steven, you've got to open your mind a little, things aren't always black and white.' There was a grumble from his companion before he continued, 'If you look at the similarities between this story and the story of Isis and Osiris ...'

'Oh come now Alex!' Steven said audibly, voice cracked with effort and frustration.

'... then Magdalene did in fact become his wife,' Alex persisted despite protest. 'This opens up the possibility that the water he turned to wine was actually at his own wedding! What an excellent way to save money on the evening do; and they couldn't even whack on a corkage charge!' He laughed as Steven, who seemed a bit cross, began to talk over the top of him.

'and ... and I suppose she lifted her skirts and showed him her vagina like Isis, too?'

'Come on, Steve,' Alex said. He stood up with an empty glass and put a hand on his friend's shoulder as he went past, 'don't sulk,' and as he walked off to the bar, 'besides it was Baubo that lifted her skirts. That's a totally different story.'

When Alex came back with a pint of beer in each hand Tabitha got up and moved to their table. She tried to steady the glass in her hand as it trembled. She had approached and drunk with men she didn't know before; some had grabbed her, some made comments about her arse, or tits, and some had used sleazy chat up lines, but she'd never felt nervous. She would retort or rebuff with ease and cheek, which would often send the offender's friends into a flurry of back slaps and laughter. These boys were different though; this was the devil she didn't know and she was unsure what she would say and how they would react. She'd noticed that Alex's bravado had increased when he saw her watching them but as she approached their table she could see him shrink and little Steven began to breathe heavily as if he was about to have an anxiety attack. She attempted to appear as passive as possible as she said, 'hi guys,' but instead felt predatory. She perched next to Alex and smiled, head turned to one side, and put her drink in front of her.

'Am I right in thinking you boys are studying to be vicars?' She regretted using the term boys, she was now a grown woman – a cougar – grooming the innocent. They nodded with reluctance. 'Well I wondered if you could help me.' Alex pulled his posture up an inch and with a fake confidence that wavered and squeaked in his voice told Tabitha they would be happy to help and then introduced himself and his friend. There followed a silence that lasted too long so Tabitha decided to wade in with the question before the situation got more uncomfortable.

'What do you know about St. Fagan?' she asked.

'You've visited the museum,' cheeped Steven, emboldened by a familiar subject and keen to prove he could speak.

'Something like that,' Tabitha replied. She was still not sure if she should mention the document; for the most part because she thought it was fiction but also because she liked to know something others didn't.

Over the next half an hour the two men began to relax and told her what they knew of St. Fagan. They had another round of drinks and discussed and debated the Saint's existence and his place within Christianity. It became clear that he was often considered more of a myth than historical fact. He didn't have a day dedicated to him like the others. It seemed Steven had done research into him in the past, due to his own curiosity after a visit to St. Fagan's village and museum. He told Tabitha that the only documentation on St Fagan was from Geoffrey of Monmouth and Geoffrey was at best a fabricator of the truth and at worst an outright liar. Tabitha asked about Deruvian too but his existence seemed even more doubtful and Alex said he had not heard of him at all.

'St Fagan is probably akin to King Arthur, or the idea that Jesus once came to Britain,' Alex stated during a pause in the conversation. Steven agreed and added that the idea of one man bringing Christianity to the country was a nice idea but could be disproved with solid historical evidence that had since been studied. 'We live in a much more comprehensive world these days,' said Alex, 'people want evidential proof of the things they're told. It comes from a greater understanding of our experience here and advances in knowledge and learning.' Steven nodded and muttered 'the forbidden fruit.'

'Do you think some things should be forbidden?' Tabitha said with a sigh, her mind now in the blue sky above them, body soft and soothed. 'I mean,' she continued when she was met with blank faces, 'if some proof was uncovered that was bad for the image of

54

Christianity for instance?' Alex assured her that there had been such things uncovered in the past but, due to its strong roots, Christianity remained.

'And,' he said, 'I suspect there are a great many more that have been hidden from view by the church that we don't know about.'

Steven added one of his now signature 'oh-come-now's' and questioned Alex's place in the clergy. 'Sometimes I think you and Nietzsche would have made excellent bedfellows.'

Alex pointed out that, if that were the case, he would not be sitting with a woman as he discussed philosophy and theology. His brow then furrowed and he turned to Tabitha to apologise for his rash comment though Tabitha had become lost in their references long before this point. Maybe she should give the document to these men, she thought, and they could take it away and study it or destroy it or whatever they wanted. It was clear they would make more of it than she ever could. Still – a tightness in her chest told her she should keep it protected. Marguerite seemed to think it was important, as did the library in Paris. Perhaps she should keep the curtain drawn for a little longer.

The conversation moved on and she let talk of St. Fagan slide in favour of personal discussions of the men's lives and studies. They both seemed like nice boys, the sort of boys she would have bullied in school, but now she felt interested in the world they inhabited. It was so different from her own. They asked her questions too and although she revealed some of herself, she kept the messy things from them. She didn't think they would like to meet a real Mary Magdalene. It had gone tea-time and she began to make her excuses and say her goodbyes when Alex felt assertive enough to ask for her name. She told them, 'Tabitha,' and Alex laughed. 'Well, all this talk of saints and we had one in our midst all along!'

It was late by the time Tabitha got home. It was dusk but the curtains were still open owing to her mum working nights. She closed them and went straight to bed. She was too tired to read but after she'd crept under the duvet and lain down she picked up the document with a lazy hand, rested it on her chest, and brushed through the pages. The scent of old perfume on the paper smelt of

Marguerite's house and took her to that dark front room and she exhaled a calmed breath.

The next morning the Reverend Geraint seemed off with her. As she worked she wondered if the smell of alcohol could have been on her breath from the evening before; she had more than she intended. When it was time to go she went to his door to be paid. His mood seemed to have improved as he thanked her and invited her in for tea and biscuits. This time she accepted and, bolstered by her conversation in the Nag's Head, asked if the vicar knew anything about St. Fagan. His brow creased for a moment to a deep set of furrows before they melted into a smile. 'Of course,' he said, 'you must've visited the museum!' She nodded and the vicar relayed a similar story to the one she had heard the day before. 'His existence is somewhat disputed,' he added. He took a sip of tea and his face raised in thought as his eyes, half shrouded by droopy papery skin, scanned the bookshelf behind Tabitha. 'The idea of a single man being responsible for bringing Christianity to our shores is interesting,' he continued, 'after all, it had to start somewhere. The faith of an individual can be invigorated by these kinds of stories, especially in this area.' He went on to explain that King Lucius had been Welsh and Faganus and Deruvianus, as they were called in Geoffrey of Monmouth's History of the Kings of Britain, had baptised the king in Wales. Tabitha kept her knowledge of the document to herself again. Once she'd read it in its entirety, she might show it to someone who could discuss it with her. Despite being the last day of her first week she avoided the pub and went straight home.

IV

Blestium

In spite of the stench, Blestium was a welcome change to the black depths of the forests and the straight road that clipped and cracked beneath the hooves of our horses. Fagan led us to an Inn, which was better than the one in Noviomagus but not by much. I left Deruvian and Fagan in the public house below and took my leave to my chamber. I sat in meditation for a while, my hands clasped together. I felt a great weight slump onto my small bones. Much of the dizziness and sickness from the forest encounter had lifted but Ciwa's presence had latched onto me, her invasive spirit hovered in the stale air.

After we left her village, we pushed through the rest of the forest and back onto a straight stony road. Deruvian kept his horse alongside mine and Fagan led in silence, the space around him absorbed the sound and energy of our movement and turned it into dead space. Deruvian chatted as we drifted along. While I had slept off the knock to my head in the village, one of the women had told Deruvian the stories of Ciwa. He now relayed these tales to me, about how Ciwa had been found as a wild woman, that she had been nursed by the wolves that ate her parents. 'That,' said Deruvian 'is why her manner seems strange.' They had also told him how the village had become comprised of only women. Before Ciwa came, when the Romans had invaded, the men had taken to the forest to fight for their freedom. They were wiped out or taken as slaves, the only males who remained were infants. With the village unguarded, the Roman soldiers moved in to take the females. Deruvian recounted the women's story; the soldiers attacked on the night of a thunderstorm. The rain pierced through the sky like blades and flung mud high into the air. The Roman soldiers knew there were only women left so they brought a handful of unskilled men. They entered the village and, despite resistance, began to take hold. Some villagers were slaughtered, and others tied up when a clap of thunder and fork of lightning illuminated black forms in the darkness beyond the boundary. One of the shapes belonged to Ciwa. In the dimness the soldiers did not know where the attack came from. The women recalled the confusion on the faces of the soldiers who had bound their wrists and ankles. The screams of several men could be heard from the edges of the clearing. Their agony split the night. At first the women had also been afraid but then it became apparent the screams of pain were only from the Romans, maybe their men had survived after all and had come back to rescue them. One woman told of the soldier who had captured her: as he disappeared towards the shouts of help another fissure of lightning tore the sky in two and she saw a huge wolf tackle him to the ground in the distance. There was no sound from him because the wolf had pulled his voice clean from his throat before he had the chance.

The storm subsided, and when the women regrouped, they met their saviour. Ciwa and her pack had been sheltering nearby when she sensed the threat of soldiers approaching. On their inspection they could see the injustice of the situation and for the first time since her removal from mankind as a baby, she had felt an empathy for her own species. She knew the pack could easily overwhelm the soldiers and came to the aid of the village.

According to Deruvian, the soldiers had made several more failed attempts on the village. When the Centurion in the region appealed to the languid Hadrian for a solution, Hadrian's lack of interest convinced him that further attacks were not worth the loss. The women showed their gratitude by placing Ciwa as head of the tribe. Although she lacked some basic social skills, she was an excellent leader and had the ability to make everyone feel important. She was also devoid of the arrogance that so often arises from leadership and was happy to ask for help when it was needed.

The account struck me as an exaggeration but my vision and Ciwa's demeanour led me to believe Deruvian in the most part.[20] I did, however, question the fate of the village without a man present. After

---

20. An exaggerated story within an exaggerated story. How on earth did she converse with them if she only had contact with wolves? Discussing the merit of this legend may be a step too far.

all, without men the women would not be able to fulfil their roles as mothers. Yes, there were some very young boys and babies still in the village, but could they survive with the gap between generations and were there enough present to avoid the sin of incest? Deruvian gave a smile. 'Well,' he said, 'did you not think it odd they left us alive following the attack in the forest? And,' he said, 'were you not confused as to why you were left behind?' At first I did not understand. It did not cross my mind that these men, these representatives of the Pope, had succumbed to temptations of the flesh outside of wedlock. I must have appeared puzzled because he continued more explicitly. He told me the women had taken both him and Fagan to help to build the new generation, so they could fulfil their roles as mothers. He said the last part slowly as if to mock my choice of words. Once they had finished what was required of them, they convinced the women to find me and reunite me with my companions.

I felt blood rush to my face, and as it did so it brought a vision of flesh and motion. I saw bare flushed body parts move against others, soft dampness against wolf skins and human hair. I heard animalistic sounds and Deruvian's shallow laugh as I became aware of my surroundings again. I felt my anger rise, how dare they sin so foully on such an important pilgrimage? How dare they do those things when I was not there? I would have stopped it. I would have stopped such filth before they were sentenced to an eternity in flames. I felt fury, but I also felt fear, I felt fear behind the disgust. I was left to sit alone in the forest whilst these men did what they did. Like a child sitting outside a brothel waiting for her father to come out.

When I was born my mother kept me from the outside world. She was not a bad woman but a woman with an ability of true sight, the same that I had inherited. She told me that when she carried me in her belly she saw that I must be kept safe, that I had a divine gift. We lived in central Italia at that time, it was a time of upheaval, of pagans moving towards the teachings of Christ. I saw very little suffering. I stayed cloistered in our house, hidden from all apart from my mother and father until the age of eleven. On the day after my eleventh birthday my usually absent father returned drunk from the tavern and beat my mother to death. I was upstairs in bed when I heard the fatal blow that made the house exhale into permanent silence. I felt mother sit next to me. She stroked my hair until the sun came up and I drifted into sleep. When I awoke, she was gone. My father told anyone who asked that she had fallen down our stone steps, drunk. My mother did not drink a day in her life, but nobody seemed to care much anyway. Then came two years of indiscriminate beatings until one day my father died after he fell down a set of stone steps whilst drunk.

Following his death, I escaped Italia to avoid the life my father had made for me. I ran to the south of Gallia, found a nunnery, and begged to join. They allowed me in, and, despite the fierceness of Mother Superior, the nunnery felt like home. The thick walls kept us cool during the summer months and protected from the cold winds of winter. I told no one of my true sight; my desire was to be the same as everyone else.

That night I sat in my inn chamber in Blestium, hands clasped, and prayed for the souls of Fagan and Deruvian. I prayed for the soul of my mother in heaven and, just as the nuns taught me, I prayed for my father's soul wherever it might be.

The morning brought a downpour. It seemed this hilly region spent much of the year in either downpours or drizzle. When Deruvian greeted me I did not look up and could not respond, the pleasantries stuck in my throat like dry earth. Outside the Inn we met with a guide. I stayed to the back of the small party with my hood up and allowed my new dutiful horse to follow the rest of the group. Today we would make our way to King Lucius's villa.

King Lucius[21] had cooperated with the Roman occupation in the early days. During those days many feared the occupation would change the way in which the Britons lived their lives. Numerous Britons fought hard to maintain their identity. It was apparent King Lucius was not one of these. At first I thought he saw the futility in resisting such a strong invading force and recognised the positive things they could bring to his people. After meeting King Lucius,

---

21.   Though in line with (that rogue) Geoffrey of Monmouth, most modern texts refute the presence of British kings during this era. Human nature tells us how unlikely it would be for conquerors to rule side-by-side with the defeated.

however, it seemed most likely that he could see the positive things they could bring to him. Things like a villa with underfloor heating.

The guide spoke very little and what he did say was in a strong accent, similar to those in Ciwa's village. It seemed this part of Britannia had a language of its own. Its people were mainly quite muscular, short, and rather hairy. This was probably due to nature of the land, their stumpy well-developed legs allowing better movement across hills and mountains. Their voices were deep and carried well across distances. As we travelled over the curves of the land, I could hear shepherds as they bellowed for their sheep, and mothers as they called their children in for breakfast, though no settlements could be seen near to where we rode.

The trip to the villa of King Lucius took the entire morning. During those hours I could not speak a word to anyone. Every so often I felt Deruvian turn to look at me. I could sense his sinful eyes burn through my cloak and onto my naked flesh. I kept my head down. I could not bear to look at him for fear that the sin might be transferred.

V

Lucius

Before I met Lucius I had an idea in my head of the kind of a person a king would be. Maybe it was unfair to expect this image to match Lucius; he was after all a king with no real power at the time. Hadrian had allowed him to keep his life and title to appease the native Britons in the area, to give them the sense that their culture would not be entirely destroyed.[22] The tactic worked to a certain extent, most of the tribes went along with the changes peaceably. As King Lucius himself explained, he was happy with the arrangement as he could retain his status but resign his responsibilities. When Lucius's father was on his death bed, the crown had been transferred to Lucius's slightly misshapen head. In Briton this was unusual as most kings were made through the murder of the previous monarch. Lucius's father, Lucius I's, throne had not been usurped in this way.

King Lucius I had been a fierce and terrifying warrior, undefeated and unmatched since he entered a life of violence at the age of fourteen. He defeated his predecessor when he was sixteen with a single blow to the face, crushing the front of his opponent's skull like an eggshell. This single blow had not been delivered by a weapon but with Lucius's own forehead.[23] After the somewhat anticlimactic victory, it was said he picked up the crown from the floor, placed it on his head, and sat on the throne as if things had always been that way. During his

---

22. This seems to give the Roman rule (or any rule in history for that matter) a kind of emotional intelligence not previously documented or supposed. Though we are aware that the Romans were somewhat unique in their intelligence and power. This doesn't seem as far-fetched as it should.

23. Geoffrey of Monmouth has Lucius's father as King Coilus and attributed his long popular rule to generosity and good deeds rather than raw, almost supernatural, aggression and power. Even in this day and age many people are more impressed by the latter.

reign very few challenged him and those who did were disposed of efficiently. One pretender tried to topple him by poisoning his huge midmorning snack. The story went that it was enough poison to despatch at least fifty men. The king admittedly felt queasy for a few days, but during these days of queasiness still succeeded in finding his would be assassin and pounding him into a thick red sludge.

King Lucius II had been unchallenged through his rule due to the notoriety of his father. The switch between Luciuses happened in private. King Lucius and his wife realised the shortcomings of their son, but loved him, nonetheless. King Lucius had attempted to train his son from a young age, push him to become a warrior like him. When it became clear he could not grasp basic instruction or movement they ceased training to restart when he was older. Even with age his abilities did not mature, and as the years went by, King Lucius I began to realise that his son would need protection of a different sort. The king's house became closed to all but essential staff. He also stepped back from his usual hands-on approach to rule so his subjects would not see him as he entered old age. When the death of the king was imminent, after his one hundred and seventeenth year, it was easier to switch the two of them without arousing suspicion. At this point Lucius the younger was past his forty-fifth year himself, and so life went on and legends began to grow of a great and immortal king of the Britons.[24]

This story had been regaled to our party by King Lucius himself whilst we ate. With his willingness to divulge the concealed information that kept him alive to any soul passing through, it was easy to see why his parents felt they needed to protect him. As well as giving Lucius his identity, the king had also left his son with a helper, Arthfael, a man who had served him with unfaltering loyalty. After the death of the queen this man kept the house running smoothly and

---

24. This does slightly line up with Geoffrey of Monmouth, however. He describes Lucius as being considered by everyone as a second Coilus. Here we see him not as a second version of his father but as a continuation. If he was so much frailer this might have been plausible, but 117? It's possible but during these times would anyone have been able to live so long?

Lucius clean, clothed, and fed. As Lucius sat with us at the dinner table, Arthfael stood at his side. He was over six feet in height and his shoulders were broad and muscular. He had the physical appearance of a man who could break bones with ease, but the care-worn look of a man who would struggle to crush a moth. After Lucius had filled us in on the secrets of the throne, he turned to Arthfael, 'isn't that right, Arth?' he said, followed by, 'sorry' as 'sorry' punctuated almost every sentence the king uttered.

Arthfael replied in a scolding tone that it was indeed correct and suggested Lucius tell the rest of the Isle whilst he had decided to confess all. 'Why not tell Hadrian?' he said, 'shall I invite him over? What do you think he would have to say about all this?' His words seemed harsh but there was no real aggression or annoyance in them. I also saw a hint of a smile on his face.

King Lucius then muttered a string of apologies without any genuine regret, 'I shouldn't have said that, sorry, sorry about that, sorry.' I could not eat much of the food King Lucius had provided. It tasted good, and I should have felt half starved, but I was still sitting in the fog of the forest and the sickness from the fall grumbled in my stomach. In the end I was glad not to have indulged as I noticed some of the food looked to be spoiled.

Once the men had had their fill, we began a tour of the villa. King Lucius led the way with Arthfael close behind, close enough to catch the king if he toppled over. There were a couple of instances of a wobble; Arthfael's strong hands came out and supported the king's elbows. The huge villa complex was undoubtably Roman. Hadrian had it built in the image of his own retreat in Tibur down to the finest details of the artwork, mosaics, and furnishings. It was clear that those who occupied it were not Roman. The villa housed hundreds of workers. They busied themselves with upkeep, cooking, and farming, which allowed the villa to be self-sufficient. It appeared to be Arthfael who oversaw the day-to-day domestic running of the household and beneath him a house manager who relayed all information to the workers. This manager had been changed thirty times in half as many years. Arthfael explained that regardless of how hard the domestics worked, they could not keep the villa in working order. King Lucius did not appear to notice, or care, about the appearance of the place. He pointed with pride to crumbled mosaics, huge cracked vases filled with spiders, and an indoor bath, slick with green slime. A thick layer of dust coated the entire villa, as if it had been empty for decades. At first, Arthfael added, the cleaners were punished for not doing their job, but when the executions resulted in no change he looked closer at the work done over a day. He found the staff slogged from sunrise to sunset. He saw first-hand, rooms cleaned to perfection by nightfall reduced to ruin by daybreak. They increased the number of staff again and again but nothing changed. At one time they had a staff member for every room, cleaning, polishing over and over again, but one by one they dropped into deep pools of hysteria, depression, and psychosis. One young woman was taken away whilst she wept and screamed about a monstrous man who wrestled her through the night and would not let her clean. Across her throat was a red-raw handprint where she said he had pinned her to the wall. Her skin was blotched purple from the effort to breathe.

The cooks faced problems too. The food we had eaten when we arrived had been brought in from elsewhere and taken into the house last minute. Food taken into the house would turn rotten in the space of a few hours. Maggots pulsated in a bowl of apples which had only been picked that day and meat butchered in the morning was rancid beyond saving by midday. The farm came with its own set of problems. Arthfael took us out of a damp mossy door to the pigpens. With calm defeat he pointed and said, 'what do you make of that?'

Deruvian chuckled as I gasped. The pigs were irregular, each one of them. Some snuffled in the dirt with two snouts or even two heads. Others sat with empty eye sockets or trotted about as numerous malformed legs trailed beneath them. The worst looked to be a combination of three pigs melted together: three heads, one smaller and almost human, seven legs and three curly tails. I put my hand over my mouth as nausea rose again. I asked why they had not released the poor creature from misery at birth. Arthfael told me that at first they had slaughtered them, but after they had killed hundreds it became obvious that disposal made no difference to the plight of the villa. They found that if they let them grow and butchered them as they would a normal pig, and ate them before the meat went bad, they tasted fine. The other animals were the same, chickens, cows, and rabbits. The fruit and vegetables also grew irregular and filled with disease. When we re-entered the building I felt faint. Il Diavolo, I whispered to myself. Fagen must have heard because he released a grunt of agreement.

I felt afraid as I was led to my room that night. In spite of the image of their sweated bare flesh locked in original sin, I wanted Deruvian or Fagen with me as the door was closed and darkness seeped into everything, even the light cast by candles. Somehow I managed to slip into an abyssal sleep, but was heaved from it in the early hours by a loud voice outside my door. I heard a, 'yes sorry, sorry,' and realised it was the king. I could hear no other voices but sensed someone else there, someone monstrous. The apologies stuttered on and reverberated off the walls of the corridor. I could find no meaning in his monologue as if half of the conversation was missing. Eventually I heard the approach of footsteps and Arthfael's voice calling Lucius several times, without 'your majesty' or 'King' attached. He then scalded Lucius in hushed tones as Lucius apologised again. I heard as they shuffled off but in the silence that followed I saw a shadow blacker than night slip beneath my door. The floor creaked beside my bed and I put the blanket over my face as sickness fingered through my entrails again.

It was not outrageous that at first I had mistaken him for Il Diavolo. Everything in the room gained weight as I gasped beneath a ton of blanket and my body sank into the bed as if composed of marble. Lead tears carved their tracks down my face and I began to beg as I choked. I started to drift out of consciousness and this is when the room around me faded and a sound scratched across the room towards me. He spoke not in sentences but in a long stream that sounded like a rush of gravel and mud, a flash flood or a landslide like the one that had enveloped half of the neighbouring town when I was a child. The words were not in the local language like Ciwa's but in Enochian.[25] I had studied the

---

25. I suspect this is where I saw the Enochian symbols in the original document. It seems they were cut from this translation, possibly because the translator only knew Latin. There's always the possibility that they believed such a language was real and felt it might have been blasphemous to use such symbols or try to interpret them into common text. As I have no leads or any ideas of who

---

language of the angels under Mother Superior, or what she had known. The rest had come to me with time, through years of conversation with light. Though this appeared to be the same language it was not composed of pure light with no shadow as I had encountered before. This was a darkness with no shadow, the kind of darkness King Solomon would have banished to a jar. However the words used were not cruel in nature, they were words of alliance and caution. Though when Mother Superior had taught me she had warned me of this. She told me that malevolent spirits will also speak the tongue of the angels, will know scripture, will be charismatic, and will appear kind. She told me that I should never trust them and if I did, I would be stripped naked and dragged through the earth to a place where I would be molested and violated for an eternity. As I lay there, I thanked Mother Superior for her insight and prayed for her soul and for mine as I chose to stand with God and the angels. I chose to be strong or was it stubborn? In the convent I had been moulded to have a rigid mind and that mind had become so central to my integrity that I ignored my own gift and judgement. I had walked into a labyrinth, a secret labyrinth lost between the mansions of God's house. Had I listened to the voice that night, I could have turned back and made my way out. At that moment the path I took would only take me to the centre and to the monster that resided there.

I still wonder whether Fagan would have been stopped had I trusted the spirit that night. Maybe if we had failed to baptise Lucius the bridge between the two might not have been built. If it had not been built, Lucius would not have obsessed over Britannia becoming a Christiandom. If he had not decided to do "God's Work" the horrors that would come to pass might have been avoided. It was difficult to believe this as I suffocated beneath the colossal weight of King Lucius I's tortured soul and tried not to listen as he growled in mutilated Enochian, do not baptise Lucius and You will bring the pits of hell to

---

might have translated it, this will remain a mystery. I deeply regret not studying the original further while I had the chance. If this is omitted what else might be? And how accurate and true to the original is the rest of this? It's adding further obscurity to an already complicated matter.

Earth – many will suffer and many will die. However genuine a demon may seem, when he begs you not to perform a baptism, it is difficult to believe him. I tried to shout, to say 'no' and 'begone foul demon', but all that came out was a pained gurgle.[26]

---

25. I always pick a particularly sequestered part of the University's library to read, study, and add notes to this document. Though I believe the Library was unaware of this document and the importance of it before I took it, and most would be put off reading it due to it being in English, I do hide it and no-one has bothered to come near me until today. It was as if he knew where I was and what I was doing. As I saw him approach I took an open book and covered the paper, as calm as I could muster. He continued to approach and I tried to convince myself that he wanted to chat me up or tell me the Library would close soon. He called my name and I looked up, shocked. 'Marguerite Martin?' he asked as he reached my table. He was in a long coat and a smart suit and seemed a little older than me. All I could do was nod and hope it was about something else. It wasn't. Luckily it seemed he was on my side. He spoke as if he was continuing a conversation we had previously begun. He said that he had tried to find the book of British kings in the archive but with no success. He laughed and said that the only way he could find it would be by taking a trip to the British Library and despite how pretty I was I would not be able to persuade him to do that as well. I tried to giggle to play along but it came out as a nervous laugh. He then came close to kiss me on the cheeks and whispered that he was sorry it was all the information he had and that I shouldn't go into the University Library anymore. He then moved away and said with more volume that it had been a pleasure meeting me. He then walked off. I sat for a moment in shock and then scrambled to get my things together and into my bag. I rushed out of the building to see if I could find him but there was no sign. In retrospect I should have played it cool. It was clear he was putting on a show in case we were being watched. As I write this I'm back in my room. As soon as I got in and sat down I began to shake, and although it has stopped to some extent I still feel dizzy and odd. I'll certainly not be back to the Library with this document and in the future I'll carry it wherever I might go. And it seems that I might be taking it to England with me. If I think about it too long it seems insane, but I've been to England before, I've been to the British Library before so it's hardly new ground and it's for research. Even though it might seem this document has developed sentience it is still a document, and I am still a researcher.

Six

It was a good start but it went south fast. There was something about free time that bothered Tabitha. If she wasn't doing something, either constructive or destructive, it began to feel as if she was in a waiting room where the main objective was to kill time. This seemed barbaric as time was an endangered species, one day it would die out, and on that day, she would mourn the time she had murdered when there was so much to spare. What was the point of a day off work sitting in front of the television only to go to bed at a reasonable time. Ferris Bueller would be appalled. She only got as far as Friday before she had to go out. She would only have a few drinks, she told herself.

It would be the start of a bender to end all benders. She was nostalgic when she messaged a few of her old friends. She remembered nights in Cardiff when things were new and full of excitement: doing shots, dancing, being hit on, standing outside to have a smoke and a chat and a laugh. The good times had stuck while the messy parts drifted into obscurity. The group met in one of their old haunts, but it didn't feel the same, or it was the same but not as she remembered. Her three friends looked tired before they even started drinking, though a couple of glasses later, and after some reminiscing, the energy levels increased. For Nicola it was the first evening she'd been away from her two young children in at least six months. Cherry spent a large portion of her time working in an ice cream factory, where her needs were not met, and the rest went to her mother who had terminal cancer. Chantelle, who Tabitha hadn't seen since they parted ways at the last session, had become a personal trainer at a local gym and had to work unsociable hours for minimum wage. There was no bitterness over Tabitha's abandonment of Chantelle during their last outing. Chantelle had also found a shag who was difficult to describe.

'His house was right in the sticks,' she said, 'and big, I mean, I probably should've got his number, dude had to have a bit – you know?' She looked wistful, 'it was just that he seemed kind of – different – in the morning.'

Nicola laughed, 'we've all been there, love, sounds like the morning after my wedding!'

Cherry cackled too but Chantelle stared ahead, 'he didn't really want to do anything either. He just sort of cuddled.'

This caused another ripple of amusement which cheered Chantelle and made her giggle. 'Maybe that was why I didn't bother with the phone number,' she added.

Tabitha sat in silence throughout; her brain felt fuzzy as a surge of adrenaline spiked through her body and fought against the alcohol. A solidity dampened the noise in the bar until all conversation had been blurred and hushed. A sound like footsteps on flagstones echoed in her ears before Cherry's voice pierced through right next to her face. She asked Tabitha if she was okay. Tabitha nodded and after a moment to orientate herself made a joke about how she'd been reading more these days and that she might be turning into a nerd. The other women chuckled and Cherry suggested an injection of tequila to cure her. They all had a shot together and the room returned to normal.

By twelve o'clock Tabitha was hanging onto Nicola's waist as Nicola tried to leave the club to get home to her babies. 'Come on!' she screamed at her, 'you can't be one of those boring mums.'

Nicola pointed out that even if she stayed she would still have to be a boring mum to look after Tabitha's drunken arse. Cherry and Chantelle then started to pull on Tabitha's arms and legs to stop her while they all laughed. In the struggle Nicola knocked over a stranger's drink and smashed the glass which caused the bouncer to throw them all out. After a loud discussion outside Cherry took it as a chance to go home too. Dark puffy rings sat under her tired eyes and she was working the afternoon and evening in the factory the following day.

Tabitha and Chantelle wandered around for a while and found another club that let them enter. It was in the cellar of a pub: small, damp, and cramped, but good music and serving until two. A thin man with long lank hair stood outside the toilets. He gave Tabitha some pills and when the bar was about to close Tabitha and Chantelle had started to come up. After they had walked the streets and spoken to everyone they came across they decided to go back to Chantelle's flat. There they finished the half bottles of spirits and holiday liqueurs in Chantelle's cupboard and argued until they forgot what the disagreement had been about. After the reconciliation they put on power ballads and sang together. With the music still on they fell asleep, fully clothed, on the sofa.

Tabitha woke up at about ten in the morning and nudged Chantelle until her bleary gummy eyes opened. After ibuprofen for headaches that felt as if their brains had been cleaved in two, they opted for a greasy fry-up washed down with hair of the dog. After this point Tabitha hit the zone. She saw it as the sort of zone people who participate in endurance sports talk about. She was on autopilot and, after Chantelle fell asleep late that afternoon, went back into town to a pub. Tabitha was low on money so stuck to stronger drinks and drank fast. By the time it got dark she was down to her last fiver. A group of men took an interest in her. They had on suits and ties which were loosened to allow them to undo the top buttons of their shirts. They smelt of sweat from a day trapped in stuffy offices and most of them had their hair slicked back with gel. After they had bought her a few drinks their limp office-worker hands began to cup and fondle her. She allowed it to continue for a while but in a moment of clarity became disgusted and walked off followed by a chorus of 'slag' and 'bitch'. When she got outside Tabitha found a ten-pound note that one of the men had stuffed into her bosom earlier. She went into the newsagents on the corner and bought a cheap bottle of spirits. The young Indian man behind the counter slowed as he took her money and before he put it in the till asked if she was on her own and whether she needed him to call a taxi. She waved an elastic arm at him and assured him that her friends were outside and they would take her home.

Tabitha drank from the bottle as she walked past packed kebab shops and drunk girls sitting on kerbs with knickers on show. After a few fights broke out nearby she decided to make her way home. The last trains were close to leaving so she snuck through the barriers and got on one that she thought would go close to where she lived. It was the right train but she fell asleep as soon as she sat down. When she woke up the train had stopped and was empty. Outside was black apart from the glow of the shelters on the platform. Tabitha felt her heart race with panic, more for fear she would be caught without a ticket than fear that she was lost. With all the swiftness she could muster she wobbled off the train. She didn't recognise the name of the place at all and the world was so distorted she struggled to read it anyway. She continued to drink from her bottle.

Tabitha's chest heaved and spluttered as a torrent of frozen water shot across her skin like pins. Someone screamed at her as she flapped her arms and struggled to surface from a cold pool she had plunged into. 'I will not let you waste your life this way!' the voice said. Her eyes were screwed shut and she gasped and tried to open them but could not. Her head was pushed under and as she came up again she coughed and gasped against the torrent's continued assault.

When she got her breath back she mustered a feeble, 'no, no, no,' as the voice said again, 'I will not let you waste your life like this!'

Her head started to clear and she could feel movement return to her limbs, enough to push her mum away for a second so she could try to stand and get out of the full bath. The first attempt failed and she slipped, plunging herself under again. She re-emerged and choked again before she managed to open her eyes. The spray from the shower crackled on the surface and she took a deep breath as the room calmed. Her mum muttered, 'I won't let you,' as she walked out of the bathroom and closed the door.

There were moments – fragments – of memory that moved into view like slides under a microscope. She remembered most of the first night though things got foggy after she'd gone to Chantelle's flat. She recalled the men she was with to get drinks and cringed. She saw herself standing over her own unconscious form on the train: hair tangled, dress dirty, heel broken on her shoe. Then there was the train platform and the sign with the name that looked as if it had been in Cyrillic. The next thing that came back was a dark field that she stumbled through until she reached a hedge. It was lit by an almost full moon and a startled rabbit made her jump as her legs collapsed. The empty bottle went into the hedge. The sun started to come up and she cried. It was daylight and there might have been a woman who spoke to her and took her phone to speak to someone. The woman was elderly and kind and sat with Tabitha and tried to make conversation. Tabitha thought she remembered the woman talk about St. Fagan's but as soon as Tabitha heard the name she got upset. She thought she might have sworn at the woman, which she felt bad about, but the memories at this point were so fragmented and vague it was difficult to make a clear assessment. The next thing she was aware of was the cold water.

Tabitha stayed in the bath, her clothes sticking to her body, until the chill got into her muscles and her hands began to cramp. She got out, peeled her dress off, and wrapped a towel around her body, which quaked and puckered. She brushed her teeth and looked at her face in the mirror. She looked worn, as though she'd aged several years in a day. It had in fact been two days and three nights; an entire day and one night was unaccounted for. It was now Monday but Tabitha didn't know that. She went into her bedroom and put on a large white cotton T-shirt that she liked to wear on duvet days. She got it in the sale, it said 'ALLSAINTS' on the front and was a size twenty so fit her like a nightgown. She lay down on her bed and as she began to drift off she heard voices from downstairs. One of the voices was her mother; the other sounded like an older woman. She could hear the kettle as it came to the boil and the sound of a teaspoon clink on the side of a cup.

When Tabitha's mum had got to the gate of the field the elderly woman was there to meet her. She apologised for using Tabitha's mobile to ring her and said she hoped she'd done the right thing. It was either call her mum or call an ambulance, but she thought an unnecessary trip to A&E would not have helped the situation. Tabitha's mum said there was nothing to be sorry about and was thankful for the help. The two women walked Tabitha out of the field and into the car. The elderly woman went with them to give Tabitha's mum a hand at the other end. When they reached the house Tabitha's mum broke into a sob and the elderly woman suggested the cold shower. This wasn't her usual style of parenting but she was happy to give it a go, if for no other reason than punishment. After they had coffee together and a chat – the elderly woman had raised three daughters two of which were equally as difficult as Tabitha – the woman refused a lift home with great firmness and left.

Tabitha's sleep was dreamless though she woke late afternoon with an echo on repeat in her head – 'I never forget to be kind to strangers' – until it had twisted around to say 'I never forget to be strange to kind girls'. A vein throbbed in her temple as she sat up. Next to her was a bottle of Lucozade and a bottle of water put there by her mum. There was also some paracetamol on her bedside table but she decided not to take them. This time she deserved the pain. She rose to her feet and felt the throb in her temple stop. She waited for the rush of nausea to hit her stomach and the sense of guilt and darkness to fill her every fibre but it didn't. Nothing ached, pulsated, or weakened. It was as though she'd spent a long weekend at a spa sitting in warm baths, on massage tables, and in saunas. She looked at her face in the bedroom mirror and saw soft, clean skin and rosy cheeks, her eyes aglow with health. It was a face that hadn't gazed back at her since her school days. She felt hungry and decided to go downstairs for something to eat.

Her mum stared at the TV and said, 'feeling a bit delicate?'

There was no concern in her voice, only veiled anger. Tabitha thought for a minute then replied, 'no… I feel … well.'

Her mum seemed a bit taken aback by the way her daughter said this – with an innocence she'd not heard since Tabitha had been a little girl – but this was overpowered by irritation. She barked, 'well that's a fucking miracle,' before she went back to watching the news.

There was no food made for Tabitha in the kitchen, no stew or soup, so she set about making some pasta with a tomato sauce that she could share with her mum. It only took her twenty minutes to prepare and she walked into the front-room and placed it in front of her mum as an offering. Her mum ate it but still wouldn't look at her daughter. She had to leave work to pick her up from a field. The fact that she had to explain that to her boss was a total embarrassment. She'd been worried for Tabitha before but never embarrassed. On the news there was a report on the rise of religious violence followed by two guests in the studio who argued over the cause of this increase. One was a female vicar and the other a man who had written many books on atheism. The atheist wouldn't give the vicar a chance to talk and spoke with fury about religion and how it caused all wars in the world. When the vicar finally did get a word in, she said that even without religion humans would find some reason to go to war, at which the atheist scoffed. She accused him of being equally extreme. He then became even more cross and pointed at her.

'You,' he said, 'you are just frightened because you realise what we are seeing here are the final death throes of religion across the globe! Have you not heard that your god is dead?'

The news reporter then interjected as it was time for the next segment but as they turned off the guests' microphones you could hear the vicar say, 'don't tell me what I think,' followed by the atheist who added, 'ha! That's rich...'

After Tabitha had eaten, she went upstairs to give her mum some space. It was odd, she'd always thought a hangover served to remind you not to drink again but although it might dissuade many for a short time it wasn't long before most would be at the booze again. This time, with her new incredible health, she thought it might encourage her to drink more but it had the opposite effect. It was a pardon, a gift of compassion too generous to waste. A part of her thought the hangover was still on its way but for now she was comfortable. She read with rejuvenated eyes.

VI

Baptismus[27]

I must have passed out. The next thing I was aware of was a strip of sunshine that leaked in through the shutters. I sat up and found I felt refreshed and well. The headache that had dogged me since the woods was gone and when I breathed in the breath was deep and filled my chest with serenity. Even as the remnants of the previous night's demon lingered and tried to finger its way into my mind, my body remained relaxed. The memory of the ordeal was tinted with fondness, an affection for the spirit who had visited. I put this down to God's strength by my side. I made my way to the banqueting hall. There was a sense of jubilation in the air, like that on a wedding day. King Lucius laughed and chatted to Deruvian with barely a pause for air. Arthfael was busy with the servants as they prepared the king's horse and bag ready for the short trip to the site of the baptism. Fagan was absent from the breakfast table at first. I assumed he was preparing himself for the baptism he was about to perform. He appeared halfway through the meal but did not eat and was sullen as usual. I hoped he had prayed for his soul and to be cleansed after the sins of the forest. I decided to reserve judgement. Only God could forgive him and if the baptism was to go ahead, I hoped God had taken mercy on him. We ate a good breakfast brought in from outside the palace, as with our previous meal. As we became full and stopped eating, the food on the table

---

27. Baptism. I write these notes as I sit on the ferry to England and I'm reminded of my own baptism. I was raised in a deeply religious house. My father died when I was a baby and my mother took it hard. She was a Christian before but after his death became devout. He had killed himself, so part of her new zeal came from her desire to pray for his damned soul and the other part was misdirected guilt. It was not her fault, by all accounts, he was an alcoholic with a gambling addiction. My mother had me baptised when I was eight by a Reverend who held my head under a bit too long. Since then I've always disliked water.

began to bruise and I watched, transfixed, as real mould unfurled and reached skyward.

When we got outside, I could see Rome had come to Britannia. The fog had cleared, and the morning was warm and golden. Our horses had been prepared for us, so we mounted and moved off. King Lucius was dressed in long white robes and his round face was ruddy and joyful. Fagan rode a little ahead of me. I had expected that he too would be suitably clad for the ritual he was about to perform but he was in his usual drab heavy garments. He took a brief glance behind and slowed his horse until mine moved to his side. I did not look up. I was still angry and filled with embarrassment over the debauchery. Fagan took a bag from the back of his horse and flung it over mine. He grunted a few words to convey that inside were robes and tools I needed to execute the ceremony that day. He was matter of fact but waited for an answer which I could not give. He asked if I understood but the only word that I could muster was 'What?' It rose like steam from the lump that filled my throat. The confusion began to shift as it made way for wrath. After how he had behaved, he now wanted *me* to do his job, the job he was sent here to do by the Pope himself. Before I could stop myself, I barked out that Pope Eleutherius had sent Fagan to do his work and I continued to chastise him even though my heart punched at the inside of my ribs. I could not stop myself until he let out an exhalation so fierce it made me jump. Without any loss of control, he told me that it was my responsibility. He then trotted-on and left me to stew.

Deruvian heard the altercation and steered his horse to ride alongside me. As usual he acted as Fagan's conscience. He excused him and apologised for him and then told me something I had not expected. Fagan and Deruvian had indeed been handpicked by Pope Eleutherius but not for the reason I had thought. Both men had been revered in Rome, not for their religious purity but for their ability to defeat any challenger put before them. They had been the emperor's property and had spent much of their youth fighting. As they grew and improved, they were made to fight before huge crowds. Here they were expected to be both bloodthirsty warriors and shrewd showmen as they took down their opponents and read the audience to decide if they should slaughter or be merciful. The pair had often fought as a duo and only against one another once. Luckily the crowd had been merciful that night and Fagan had allowed Deruvian to live.

Pope Eleutherius had been very specific that the role of Fagan and Deruvian should be kept a secret. It was important that no one should find out that I was the virgin who would perform the baptism. The Pope was paranoid that Britannia would rise against Christianity and kill me before I could get to the king. Why then had I not been told? I had, it seemed, in a letter that I had not received. Pope Eleutherius had sent a private messenger, but the road from Rome is treacherous and saturated with temptation so he may have been killed or coaxed to a spiritual demise. It read like a comedy of errors. Fagan and Deruvian assumed I knew and was playing my part in the ruse, but all the while I was unaware that the men with me were for my protection alone and were damned beyond retribution before we had even set foot in foreign lands. For the rest of the journey our party remained silent whilst King Lucius and Arthfael stayed at the head of the group, a torrent of monologue flowing from Lucius all the way.[28]

The large well was in a clearing of a wood owned by the king. Lucius officially owned the 8000 acres around his villa, also gifted to him by Hadrian. The local population, however, may not have seen it as such and according to Arthfael, Lucius had never studied the maps or cared much about his estate. As we dismounted and walked into the clearing my body relaxed. The bones in my shoulders and spine sighed and

---

28. This all seems odd. Granted this would be a reason for the document to be hidden from view by the Church, but it sits strange. It would go against all we know about the history of Christianity. There are still cultures which won't allow women to speak casually in church, let alone give sermons or perform rights. And even if they did allow a woman to perform baptisms at this time, why was she of all people, chosen? She does have some kind of gift, but if we look back at other cases this would be more likely to get her tied to a stake and burnt rather than bring her job prospects.

Even if this is a piece of the puzzle put into place, after all the Church would not want it to be known that Christianity was brought to Britain by a woman, we can't forget the document is still only the dictation of a ghost to a clairvoyant in the dark ages. What are they afraid of? I can understand why they might have hidden it when it was first written but there are very few people who would believe such a document to be genuine in this day and age.

cracked in the warm sunshine. I inhaled as if it was the first time I had done so since we reached this pagan land. The birds twittered in the trees and there was a low lazy vibration of insects in the air. The world smelt fresh and alive. God was here.

Despite the warmth of the day, the source of the well was deep in the earth and the coldness of the water bit at my ankles and legs. I felt giddy as I walked further in to waist height. I gasped and tried hard not to let my teeth chatter. I and King Lucius had donned white robes and as I stood ready, Bible in hand, he placed a foot into the water and screamed. Arthfael, who was beside him, spoke a few words of encouragement in a gentle voice as he realised how cold it was when he saw me enter. All that came from Lucius was another scream and, 'Sorry, no, ssssorry no!' The look on his face was not one expected from the pain of cold water but one of absolute fear. He then pointed above my head. The others looked to where he pointed, and I saw from their expressions that something was not right. I glanced at Fagan and saw a momentary shock flash across his face, which was enough to tie my stomach in a knot and my blood to run icier than the water that surrounded my body. Now my teeth chattered mercilessly against each other and my skull reverberated with each impact.

'What is it?' I managed to breathe. But the others stood motionless and soundless apart from the staccato whimpers from Lucius. That was when I lifted my chin and saw two filmy eyes looking back. Translucent tentacle hair drifted around a face and my shoulders. Where the neck would be was a fold of ragged delicate tissue. Despite the hideousness of the vision, when I looked at that head, I was not afraid. It spoke to me.

It said, *When I live, I am Albanus of Verulamium. I live to be martyred for the defence of a priest in Britannia. I live to die so that others will not suffer by Roman hands. I am a messenger of God. You must perform this baptism for the good of my people in the future and for all Christendom.* Then the head vanished, and a light shower of water wetted my forehead.

So that was the miracle. The miracle that made Pope Eleutherius canonise Fagan following his fevered death ten years later. It turned out that Fagan and Deruvian were not only there to make sure nothing happened to me, but also to act as a powerful visual front to the mission we achieved in Britannia. Once Albanus of Verulamium had vanished, the ordeal slipped from King Lucius's memory without a trace. He entered the well with a gleeful giggle at the chilly water. I performed the baptism, read the scriptures, anointed the king, submerged his wriggly form, and patted his back as he coughed and spluttered out the water that had gone up his nose.[29]

After the ceremony we made our way back to the villa. King Lucius seemed thrilled by his initiation into the one true faith and talked without pause to the door. The other men were quiet. The vision at the well had shaken them. Even Fagan seemed on edge. I had ridden alongside Lucius and Arthfael on our return. At one point, Arthfael turned from the chatting king and asked me in a hushed voice whether he had seen what he believed he had seen. I affirmed his vision. He asked what it was and whether it was a bad omen to see a detached head float above a king. I told him that in this case it was not. I told him that it was the head of a future martyr, that what we achieved today would be felt in Britannia for centuries to come. He was not comforted by my explanation. Since our arrival at the villa, it had not escaped my attention that Arthfael was not happy with the king's religious conversion. His full obedience appeared to be to his king and that still may nave been King Lucius I. Even if he would not say it aloud, I saw his reservations as we planned the baptism. Usually, if Lucius wanted to do something Arthfael would help satisfy his 'whim'. I told him, as he puzzled over the ethereal head, that the baptism was not something done to placate his majesty, that it was a solemn affair that, especially on this occasion, held much gravity and importance. We travelled the rest of the way apart.

Before we got back to the king's villa, clouds had swept in from the west and Britannia became grey again. With the clouds came a wind that pierced the skin and gnawed at the bones. When we arrived the fires had been lit and the housekeepers worked hard to keep them

---

29. So according to this they later changed who performed the baptism. Which begs the question, why send her in the first place?

---

alight as they brought wood in from outside the gates so that it would not rot before it was needed. Again, we ate well that evening, a celebration for the day's triumph. I felt a different air in the house from when we had left that morning. It was that of a foot lifted off a mouse a moment before it would be crushed. Sure enough, after we had finished eating the food left on the table remained good, edible, no rot or disease to be seen. King Lucius called it a miracle of the baptism. I agreed. Arthfael kept quiet on the subject, Deruvian played along, and Fagan, as always, remained an observer.

As we went to our chambers that night, Arthfael left the side of the king and requested to speak to me. The freshness of the food had made him worry. He looked older than he had before; the vision at the well had shocked more white into his hair and further furrowed his brow. I assured him that the freshness of the food was God's way of showing the righteousness of our actions. He was unconvinced, he felt the memory of King Lucius I had faded. Again, I reassured him that this was a good thing. The king's memory had solidified in the villa and had become tactile and dangerous. I told him what we had done had no doubt pleased his restless soul and allowed him to pass from our world and into the next. Arthfael grumbled his qualms. He thought King Lucius I had finally given up, after years of trying to keep his kingdom intact, his attempts to push his son away from Roman bribes, and this impulsive action that would now further remove the new king from his roots.

'Sir,' I said sternly, 'I must insist that this baptism was no whim of your king's.'

With that I went into my chamber and closed the door. I heard Arthfael's footfall move up the corridor and I was left alone in a darkened room. My light cast shadows that leapt about on the walls as I stood motionless. It felt empty, like a question with no response. I waited a while for a reply, but none came. I spent some time in prayer. Where I would feel a surge of wonder and connection to God, I felt only the emptiness of the room. I prayed longer than most nights, waiting, inviting that majesty, but after an hour of stillness I got to my feet and went to bed. At this time I was not afraid. It was possible the demons that had been there had affected the villa in some way. I went to sleep without trouble and for the first time in my life awoke the next day without having had a single dream.[30]

---

30. It feels that although there is a shadow of existence of these characters, King Lucius, St Fagan, and Deruvian, it is difficult to present any real evidence of them. If this was indeed a genuine cover up from the Church it seems they might try harder to make them more believable. Give them their own saints' days, etc.

I arrived at Dover last night and took a train to central London. As soon as it was morning I went to the British Library and waited outside for the doors to open. As I entered I was pleased to see that the man at the main desk was only an assistant librarian. The managers of these places seem to know too much. He wasn't sure about the document and suggested he fetch a more senior member of staff. I told him that there should be files on the document somewhere as it was quite important. He went away to look and I sat and waited nearby. The library was quiet, only a few scholars wandered here and there with piles of dusty books. At first the peace was welcomed, I felt a sense of calm, but as time lengthened I started to worry. He had been gone for almost half an hour and I had begun to suspect the worst when finally I saw his smiling face bounce towards me. He was excited as he approached. As he spoke to me he lowered his voice and told me that the notes I had asked about had been in a part of the library he had not been in before. It had been a part of the library that held notes and documents that were not for the eyes of the general public. He had thought that he shouldn't tell me but he said that I seemed to know quite a lot about it and he wasn't really sure historical documents such as this should be kept secret. People deserved to know the truth about their history, he said. He then told me that they didn't have the document there, which I already knew, but that it had gone to the Louvre who had then passed it on to the Bibliotheque de Paris, which I also knew. I didn't want to dishearten him so I thanked him for the information and tried to share in his enthusiasm. I then asked him if he knew who had sent it to them originally. He did, it was the Welsh National Museum in Cardiff and he thought that this had been the original source of the document. He said there was a letter from the National Museum of Wales in the file resisting the removal of the document from their archives. It seemed it had a lot of historical importance to Wales and they felt it should remain with them. This prompted a letter from the Vatican, which the assistant librarian said was rather stern and threatened legal action. The Welsh National Museum, being only small, had no choice but to send the document away but they weren't happy with it and sent another letter to that effect with the document.

With all this in mind I went straight to Paddington station and booked tickets to Cardiff for tomorrow morning. The assistant librarian had asked me if I would like to meet up later so he could show me around central London and take me to dinner. He was quite attractive and sweet and ordinarily I might have taken him up on his offer but I thought it would be better for him if he was not associated with me after what had happened in the Bibliotheque de Paris. I politely declined and told him that I would be leaving for France. As I went to go I thought again about his safety and turned and said quietly that it might be best if he didn't mention my visit to his boss as I had some issues at previous libraries. He became animated again, thrilled by the cloak and dagger, held up a three fingered boy scout salute and promised he wouldn't breathe a word. His lightness to the situation put everything into perspective for a moment and I laughed and regretted even more now that I couldn't spend more time with him.

Seven

Due to her flexible hours, Tabitha could shift her week one day on without suspicion. Reverend Geraint mentioned her Monday absence when she turned up on Tuesday but only due to his interest at what she'd done over the long weekend. She told him that she hadn't done much – relaxed and recovered from three days of gardening. She admitted that she wasn't as fit as she thought and that she had ached. He agreed that gardening could catch you unawares that way.

'But despite that, you are looking well from it!' he commented.

'I feel well,' she said and smiled. It was a real smile and she'd not lied, she did feel well.

On Thursday the Reverend set up a cosy afternoon tea for Tabitha and three of the churchwardens he wanted her to meet. She shifted in her chair and took less sugar in her tea than usual. All three were well-dressed ladies in their mid to late seventies. They asked her questions about her life and where she saw herself in the future. When she replied they leaned forwards in their seats to listen and nod with intent. At first Tabitha told them there wasn't much to tell, but from their expectant faces it was clear they knew about the CBO and why she had been placed at the church for work. They sidestepped any direct questions about her misdemeanours but asked if she had a husband or boyfriend.

'I did have a long-term boyfriend,' she said, in a bid to conceal other information she knew they wouldn't approve of by volunteering something more palatable, 'but it wasn't a good relationship for me.'

'Why was that, dear?' asked one of the ladies who had her hair trussed up so neatly she looked like a retired ballerina.

'It was unhealthy,' she offered but they waited for more. 'He was abusive ... he hit me,' she said.

The women broke into a cacophony of intakes of breath, sighs, and tuts and then chirped about how brave, sensible, and grown-up she had been to leave him. It was best she kept quiet about her mother's disapproval, she decided, and that she should have listened to her and not moved in with him in the first place. They seemed satisfied with the story Tabitha had provided and unanimously decided these hardships were why Tabitha had got into trouble with the police. The conversation then moved on to Marguerite and her garden. One of the women claimed she knew Marguerite from her knitting circle. She described her as a kindly old woman who loved knitting and socialising and who made the best marmalade she'd ever tasted. By her description Tabitha thought it must have been a different Marguerite. She couldn't imagine Marguerite enjoying a chinwag let alone being a member of a knitting circle. Tabitha told them about the steep slope, the weeds that had overrun the borders, and soil thick with clay. They praised Tabitha for her grit and determination and told her how impressive it was that she'd helped Marguerite so selflessly.

'The time you spent with her before she died must have meant a lot to her,' the lady with the neat hair said.

'That's right,' the lady who claimed to know Marguerite added, 'the end of someone's life can often be a lonely time.'

As the tea came to an end the third lady, who seemed the oldest of the three, with her spine bent into a gentle curve, filled a natural silence with talk of the late summer Bank Holiday that weekend. The lady with the neat hair said that the forecast was awful.

'Typical!' said the eldest lady as she threw her hands to the sky, 'and the weather has been so good otherwise, and I was planning to go to the food festival at the St Fagans Museum with my son.'

The moment his name was mentioned, Tabitha's heart fluttered like it used to in school when someone mentioned a boy she fancied. As the women continued to talk about the museum, her pulse lowered but her calm had shifted and she struggled to retrieve it as it slipped further from her reach. Her focus phased back in as she realised the older women had asked her if she'd ever been to the museum.

'No,' she said, to secure an answer, before she realised she'd already told the vicar she had. 'I mean yes,' she corrected to a room of frowns. 'I visited when I was a child but can't remember much.'

'Well, you must go again,' said the Reverend with conviction. They all agreed that she must go again. 'Especially as the site is in continuous change. They're always adding historical buildings and new events.'

'And the gardens are beautiful,' said the lady with the neat hair, 'as a gardener it would be a crime for you not to go and experience them.'

Tabitha told them she would visit soon because she wanted to move away from the subject. It gave her an odd compulsion to leave – to go back to her room, pick up the manuscript, and slip into the ancient landscape. It was almost like homesickness: a longing for those words that she now saw as a physical memory.

As she got on the bus that afternoon, and watched the grey road, and the grey sky, and the grey people, she started to think maybe she should go to the museum. Perhaps she could bring some of the world in those pages into the present. That night, as she lay in bed, she decided she would go the next day. Afterwards, she lay awake for more than an hour in anticipation.

The seasons had shifted overnight. On the bus the next morning she watched through the wet glass as rain marched across the fields in solemn columns. The heaters were on but some passengers towards the front were too warm so had opened the upper windows. The rain found its way through and licked across Tabitha's face every so often. She'd thought she might stay at home but realised the museum might be quieter on a miserable day. The bus emptied and when it got to the village, Tabitha was the only person left onboard. She thanked the driver as she got off but he didn't acknowledge her. She put her hood up and walked through the museum entrance.

Inside the one-hundred-acre grounds stood historical buildings from all over Wales: dismantled, reconstructed, and decorated to reflect the age in which they were built. The buildings differed wildly from small cottages comprised of whitewashed coastal boulders to a working men's club from the nineteen-twenties. There was a medieval prince's court and even a small cockfighting arena. The effect was not one of travelling through time to various eras but more of non-linear time that stood side by side and grouped into pockets like vegetables in an allotment ready to be picked. Tabitha wandered in silence from place to place. The grounds were close to empty of visitors. The trees breathed and shook their leaves in the gusts and the sheep in the central field sheltered against the hedge. There was something sullen but relaxed about the whole experience. As the day wore on the rain started to soak through her trousers and as the paths became wetter her shoes also started to leak.

Inside each building was a member of staff who would answer questions and make sure no one broke anything. As Tabitha walked past the dark window of a mill in a copse she saw the glow of a mobile phone and the bored face of a young woman who hadn't seen a sightseer all shift. Tabitha followed a trail through the wooded area and reached a cluster of roundhouses with mud walls and straw roofs. She went in and found them empty; maybe the staff member had gone for a break and forgotten to lock it or maybe they assumed visitors wouldn't bother to walk that way in the wet. There was no artificial light, the only illumination came through the door from outside. The earthy smell of smoke and soot from the fire penetrated the air. She sat on a low seat covered in a fur blanket and wondered if she would be allowed to do so if the staff member had been present. Although the fire in the middle of the roundhouse was out, some residual warmth remained and she could feel the damp that had got through her clothes warm and start to dry. She felt three days of gardening caress her body in waves of quiet ache and she yawned as the shadowed interior soothed her eyes. She heard someone outside the door as she began to drift off and the sound of a padlock click shut. It crossed her mind to call out but she didn't intend to move and she felt sure they would be back soon, they could be going to eat lunch. She started to dream – or what seemed like a dream as she felt she was awake, in part.

She was in a bathtub with no toys, which she'd been in for a very long time. The water had gone cold and there were no bubbles. She tried to get out but she was too small. She managed to climb up on the side but her wet feet slipped and as she fell, she cut her head open on the corner of the bathroom door. The blood mixed with the water in her hair and ran down her face and she began to cry. She went downstairs a step at a time, her bare bum on the scratchy carpetless boards. When she got to a living room, she saw plastic patio furniture around and a man asleep on a dirty rug. He looked white with big black rings around his eyes like a panda. She tried to wake him up but couldn't, so put her raincoat on to try to warm up. Then she was sitting on the same dirty rug. She felt uncomfortable and realised her knickers were wet and so was the rug. She wore a pink dress with a little dog on the front. The little dog was ugly and misshapen but she liked the dress and she felt sad when she realised she had got wee on the dress as well. A grown-up she didn't know came into the room accompanied by her mum and dad. It was a man who seemed very tall and big, not thin and pale like her mum and dad. He crouched down beside her and looked at her in the face and smiled. He reminded her of playing out in the sun with her brothers and sisters and of their neighbour who would invite her in and give her a cup of tea in a floral teacup and feed her cake and biscuits. She smiled back. He then asked her, 'would you like to come with me, Tabitha?' and she smiled and nodded. There was no sound from her parents as she was led out gently by the hand instead of a hard drag by her arm.

She heard someone shout her name and the roundhouse came into focus. She sat up to hear where the voice had come from but it didn't call again. She relaxed as her mind tried to piece itself back together. The images had seemed real, like a recollection or even as if she'd only experienced it in that moment. The rain now fell heavily on the roof and to her side a leak ticked onto the dirt floor. The level-headed healthiness she'd felt for the last few days evaporated and underneath sat the same rot, like a dead bloated fat toad beneath a stump. She heard the padlock click again and the wooden door opened. She could see a silhouette against the frame of the door with the light behind them. The staff member jumped as she saw Tabitha's form on the chair.

'What on earth?' the figure said with initial anger and then with delicacy, 'I'm terribly sorry, I had no idea you were in here.'

'It's fine,' said Tabitha, though her voice betrayed her sudden drop in mood. She got up to leave but the woman stopped her at the door.

'Look, let me make it up to you,' she said and promised Tabitha vouchers for the giftshop.

Tabitha spent about fifteen minutes browsing the gift shop. The woman had been generous with the vouchers and Tabitha toyed with the idea of buying a bottle of locally made gin but picked out some Welsh pottery to give to her mum instead. She'd not managed to reconcile with her since the events of the weekend. After she bought her peace offering and had it wrapped with care at the till, she walked to the gardens that surrounded the Elizabethan mansion at the other end of the grounds. As she approached, the path opened out and two large square ponds sat on either side. The water from one rushed beneath a bridge and into the other which was set lower in the surroundings. She stood for a while and watched the drizzle as it hit the surface and caused circular ripples to rush outwards before they vanished again. At the furthest point of the pond a heron stood on one leg. Tabitha hadn't seen one in real life before and hadn't realised from pictures in books how distrustful and cantankerous they were. The heron examined her as she looked at the ducks and coot and when she glanced over again its face was venomous. Uncomfortable with the scrutiny, she decided to move on but as she did so the large bird took flight and screeched as it went: a stream of heron expletives at the inconvenience Tabitha had caused.

The garden was sad in the downpour. The heavier later-flowering perennials drooped their heads under the weight of the shower while most of the rose petals lay battered on the floor. A shadow of what she experienced in the roundhouse followed her. Unlike her dreams, the more she thought about it the more it moved into reality. She entered a tunnel of hedging that bridged the path and thought she saw a small child in a raincoat run across the path on the other side. When she emerged, she saw no sign of anyone.

She left the museum disappointed. She'd gone there with the belief that she would make some kind of connection with St Fagan, though she had no idea how that could have happened. The only thing she'd come back with was the bloated toad in her soul – which she thought she had left in a field last weekend – and a new enemy in a heron. She took the bus and got back home cold and soggy. Her mum was still at work so she put the present on the kitchen table and went upstairs to have a warm shower. After she'd showered she put on her pyjamas and lay on her bed. Her mum must have washed and dried the bedsheets; they were fresh and crisp. She put her face in her pillow and felt as though she wanted to cry but couldn't. Even after her shower Tabitha could smell the smoke of the roundhouse in her hair and the vision flicked through her mind like pages of a book. It wasn't just the incident in the roundhouse either, there were other thoughts that opened and expanded in her mind. There was a broken plastic slide in a garden full of dog shit and a step outside a house where she sat, her face and hands sticky and dirty. It was as though these thoughts, or memories, as they now appeared, were painted fresh onto her brain as she lay there. They became enriched with smells, sounds, and feelings, she could hear constant barking as she tried to sleep in a room with no curtains, the streetlight outside as bright as daytime.

The man sat her in the back of a car, put a seatbelt across her, and snapped it in place. The car was new and had all kinds of lights and buttons inside. She stared up out of the window at the tops of houses and saw them reduce to a beat of house, no-house, house, no-house, house, no house until all she saw was the stretched branches of trees full of leaves. The wet in her knickers had gone cold and had begun to make the seat damp which made her feel ashamed. She could see the man's face in the mirror if she sat up really straight: a rough chin and downturned lips which she assumed were unsmiling because she had got pee on his backseat.

After ages the tyres crunched over a gravel drive and the man got out and said, 'I'll only be a minute, sweetie,' before he closed the door and left her alone. There was a dead silence apart from a few clicks from the car as it cooled. She felt safe inside, cocooned. But her cocoon was torn through when a woman opened the door with a huge smile and began to compliment her as she took off her seatbelt and led her out by the hand.

'What a beautiful, brave girl you are,' she said, 'and what a pretty little dress.' Tabitha blushed, not from the compliment but because she had ruined the dress and it was a matter of time before they found out and took her back to the dirty rug. They didn't take her back to the dirty rug though, they took her to a huge house with great trees and giant grasses out the front. As they walked through the doorway, she saw glimpses of children as they peeked through bannisters and ran from room to room playing. The grownups took her into a big room that had dark wooden panels on every wall and a dark wooden desk that was taller than her. There was another woman and a man sitting opposite the desk. The woman looked at her with such warmth that Tabitha thought she must have known her but had forgotten. Afraid that her forgetfulness might be found out and she would be taken home, she let go of the woman's hand who had led her there, went straight to the new woman, placed her cheek on her lap and looked up into her eyes with an attempt to convince her that she knew exactly who she was. That was when Tabitha saw tears glimmer on the woman's cheeks and assumed the gig was up. She must have realised Tabitha had neglected to remember her and was upset. Tabitha patted her hand to rectify this and the other adults in the room cooed and made comments about how sweet she was.

Well, the woman must have forgiven her because Tabitha was taken back to the womens house. The house was next to lots of other houses, like where Tabitha lived but it was quieter and the front gardens had lawns and neat flower beds instead of rubbish and old mattresses. Inside the house she was given her own room with a small bed covered in a pink sheet and a duvet that smelled of washing-powder, unlike the one she had at home which was stained and smelled of cigarettes. The woman put Tabitha into a warm bath full of bubbles, drying her carefully afterwards, and then put her into pyjamas. They ate together at a table with the man who had sat next to the woman in the wood-panelled room earlier. They had fish fingers, mashed potatoes, and peas. Tabitha especially liked the tomato sauce and dipped the fish fingers in it and mixed it with her mashed potato, which gave it pretty red swirls. That night she lay down and then it was morning. She saw nothing of the night; there were no barks or shouts that woke her up; it was as though no time had passed and she'd not been to sleep at all. The woman came in, got her up and dressed, and then gave her cereal and milk. She never had food in the morning at home; sometimes she wouldn't be given anything to eat until the late afternoon.

This went on for what seemed like a while. Eating at least three times a day, regular baths, whole nights of sleep in her own comfortable bed. At first she wondered when they would take her home and she worried about it because she didn't want to go home. Every so often she would think about her mum and dad and feel a bit sad but after a while she forgot what they looked like and then who they were and then she couldn't distinguish them from the mum and dad she now lived with. It wasn't long after that she stopped thinking of them and her old home and the journey in the car as they folded into her new memories and became nothing more than a visit to someone else's house or any other car trip.

One day her dad left. She had only heard her mum and dad argue once and the rest of the time they didn't seem to speak much. He spent some time with Tabitha and she cried sometimes when he went to work as if he would leave forever but she wasn't as close to him as she was to her mum. After he left and was not sleeping at the house anymore, he would come and see Tabitha now and again but this became less and less and eventually, after she started school, he didn't come and see her anymore and Tabitha's mum didn't talk about him. If her friends at school asked about her dad, she said she didn't have one and that is what it felt like, not that he'd gone away but that he'd ceased to exist. It didn't really bother her that she didn't have a dad.

VII

Adlais

Here I could have departed Britannia. I might have made my way home and lived the remainder of my life content with the role I had played in the history of an island turned from barbarism to religion. I had not managed to rid myself of the void that had entered me in my chamber after the baptism. Even after I left the villa and King Lucius's land I still had no visions, heard no souls speak or confide in me, felt no warmth from the hands that had protected me through my life, and saw no light in a persistent grey sky. It was as though I had been severed from Him. It was fear that kept me in Britannia. When I took my final breath on that island, I remembered the sunshine of Roma.

The year that followed the baptism was welded hard with rust in my brain forever. I spent much of the first months at the king's side as his religious advisor of sorts. King Lucius was excited after his baptism, and with his excitement grew an insistence that every one of "his" subjects should experience the same. Arthfael spent most of that time in attempts to downplay the event as he tried to move the king's attention to other endeavours. However, when he did persuade the king to hunt, fish, or look for treasure, on a mock antiquated map Arthfael had made himself, all the king could speak of was the whole land's conversion to Christianity. At first Arthfael's negativity and quiet undermining vexed me. I attempted to sabotage him with my own enthusiasm which was often met with a sigh. A few times Arthfael had escaped the villa with the king without me. When this happened a few days in a row, I ensured I spoke to King Lucius at dinner each night to ask him if I could accompany him in whatever activity was planned for the next day.

One evening, after we had eaten, Arthfael knocked on the door of my chamber. It was so soft, that at first I thought that someone had rapped on a door further up the corridor. When I did not answer he called through to me. My name was gentle on his tongue. I found it difficult to pinpoint Arthfael's age. He must have been quite old because of the years he had served Lucius I and his son, but there was a youthful look in his eyes and his body was strong. He was not aggressive with me that night, he was rarely aggressive, but his words shook me as I tried to disregard them. He told me he knew the Lucius line better than he knew his own kin and even though Lucius II might seem weak and stupid, the blood of his father was in his veins and that was what made Lucius II more dangerous than his father. Lucius often had the intensity and drive of his father but lacked direction and sense. With the gifts he had received from the Romans, Lucius also had the means to make any whim a reality, and if that boulder began to roll there was nothing, Arthfael said, he could do.

'I saw his father in the same flurry of excitement before war,' he told me. 'If we let this continue, the blood and suffering of many will be on your hands.'

I assured him that God would not allow any such thing to happen in his name. I tried to ease his mind with what I understood to be the warmth and love of the Lord but he shook his head and called me naïve.

'You might know religion,' he said, 'but I know people, and war is what we are heading for.'

I told him that a holy war was not something we should shy from. Something changed in him at that point; I saw a decisive look flash in his eye as his chest expanded and his muscles began to engorge. I cowered and hid my face. I may not have had a spiritual connection to his soul as I would have had before, but at that point I knew he wanted to beat me to death. I do not know what changed his mind but when I was brave enough to look, he had disappeared and shut the door behind him. It had not been a threat; he would have killed me. I realised at that point that the baptism had put the boulder in motion; maybe he had seen the same.

I stayed in the villa from then on. After the ceremony was completed, Fagan and Deruvian spent their time sitting around the villa, drinking and playing ludus latrunculorum, often for coins that swung from one to the other with no real gain for either man. Fagan relaxed now that the work he had been paid for was done. He remained sullen and uncommunicative but on occasion would say hello if we were in the same room. I asked Deruvian one afternoon why Fagan seemed different now the baptism was over. He told me Fagan was a man who did not suit peacetime, without a fight he would get grumpy. I asked him what fights he had in the villa to keep him happy. Deruvian gave a sly smile and told me that it was the fight he anticipated that made him happy. He patted my shoulder as he got up and congratulated me. Like Arthfael, he had already pinned the blame on me.

In retrospect I can see when it all began, though at the time it had seemed like any other peculiar day in Britannia. I woke up and washed. The bathroom was open for anyone to walk in so I would take water into my room and wipe down with a cloth. I always brought in cold water from the outside well. The water in the villa came through pipes and was heated by fires. Though the instances of rot, decay, and deformation had stopped, I preferred not to use anything from the villa unless it was a necessity and the water from the pipes smelt strange, ever-so-slightly of sulphur. After my ablutions, I went to the Sacrarium. When the Romans built the Sacrarium, it had been a shrine to a pagan god. An altar remained in the middle, its stone carved with bunches of grapes and horned demons. On the slab top lay the scriptures. A large polished wooden cross leant against the back wall and a tapestry depicting Christ's crucifixion hung above. I knelt on a red cushion and prayed. I had been reluctant to use the Sacrarium at first, owing to its pagan roots, but after the baptism and my loss of connection to Him, my desperation drew me. In truth it reminded me a great deal of the chapel at the nunnery. That morning I prayed furiously, as I had every day I spent in the king's villa. It was not until I felt my stomach grumble that I noticed it had passed midday. This was odd as usually I would be disturbed at some point by a maid, some other resident of the villa, or the king himself. I ventured out, in the most part to look for food but also to find another human being.

The villa appeared deserted. No one cleaned, or fetched and carried, or cooked, and I saw no sign of the four men. I began to walk the corridors and rooms as I searched for someone. I wandered at first, but the longer I looked the more briskly I moved, until I broke into a jog, and into a run. That is when I started to call out 'Hello,' then, 'Is anybody there?' Sweat trickled down to my chest and I held back tears. I collapsed on a chair and was about to weep when I heard the front door bang and the sound of feet rush through the passageway. I leapt up, half concerned, half relieved. A man dashed into the room. I did not recognise him. He was in leather armour that seemed dark and wet in places and creaked as he snatched at my arm. I pulled away as the smell of iron caught in my nostrils.

He said, 'You must come now, where you can be safe.'

I couldn't respond and, with only the concern in his face to trust, I followed behind as we scampered through the villa and out the back entrance.

The man took me through the immediate grounds and into a grotto I had not seen before. Inside it was like the Sacrarium, except that here the pagan paraphernalia remained. A winged woman stood in the centre; her one outstretched arm gripped a laurel wreath as she gazed heavenward. One muscular leg had escaped her robe and her chest was broad and full of pride. I perched at the statue's base and tried to get my breath back. The soldier looked over at me, wild-eyed, and let out a burst of laughter. It was the laugh of a boy playing armies in the streets with his friends; the boy that had found the best hiding place. I felt as though I should tell him off, to say that I failed to see the funny side, but my heart betrayed me and I giggled too. After we had stopped breathing so hard, he lunged over and kissed me, very sweetly, on the cheek and ran back out. The front of my clothes were sticky with blood. I wanted to feel disgusted. I put my hand on my cheek, it was hot.

I was only in the grotto a few minutes before Fagan sauntered in and said, 'Let's go.'

Whatever upset had happened was over now, and it was safe for me to return to the building. I asked after the soldier, but no one seemed to know or care who he was. Lucius had a regiment assigned to him, a mixture of soldiers from Roma, Britannia, and other lands that the Romans had travelled. Some had gone willingly, mercenary types, and some were taken and broken in to their new lives once they lost sight of their homes and everything familiar to them. They lived in barracks on the king's land and were strong enough in number and skill to keep local tribes, who had decreased in size over the last ten years or so, at

96

bay. These barracks were the assurance Lucius needed to do as he pleased in the area. It was clear, however, that Lucius lacked the military aptitude to lead assaults on the villages that opposed the new compulsory worship of the one true God.

When we began God's mission proper, I was eager to be involved. The men used a chamber off the main kitchen to plan. Here it was decided who would be targeted for religious enlightenment and conversion. Hadrian had given King Lucius a large map that showed the outlying settlements in the locality. He was also given writings that detailed the nature of the inhabitants of each community. Ciwa's village was included, along with grave warnings about the size, strength, and ferocity of the women who lived there. I could not remember the women in the village being as large, muscular, or abnormal as the notes suggested. The first villages the men tackled were those described as friendly, then those compliant, those that were non-compliant, then the hostile inhabitants.

I travelled with the men to the first wave of friendly groups. All were basic, not unlike Ciwa's tribe. They lived in dark round mud huts with earthen floors. They would defecate in the woods and wash in the streams and rivers nearby. They would hunt and gather food from their surroundings. We arrived accompanied by a small group of soldiers in case we were met with any resistance or to deter resistance. I would load my horse with scriptures and artefacts. All of these villages had come into contact with King Lucius's soldiers or Hadrian's soldiers at some point and the initial targets cooperated without fuss. The men would get the entire tribe to gather, and I would speak of the greatness of God. We would bring a trained translator from the villa as many only spoke the native tongue. These translators would often stay to teach Latin and continue to read from the scriptures. Most of these natives had been coerced into worshipping the pagan idols of the Roman empire during the initial occupation so, although these pagan idols were not unlike their own, moving to worship the one true God was not such a big step.

During one such visit I stood, as usual, and read the scriptures. Fagan, behind the group I preached to, went into a roundhouse with a man and woman. Before I had finished, I saw him emerge with a young girl. She clung onto his elbow as if he were her father and looked up at him with adoring dark eyes. As they walked towards us the woman, who I assumed was the girl's mother, came back out and called, her face wet with tears. The girl did not take her gaze off Fagan. The man hurried after the woman and took her back into the hut. When I had finished my sermon Fagan brought the girl to me. Her name was Adlais, and she wanted to travel with us to help spread the word of God. The men had decided that having a native at our side would influence how the others received us.

The people in the compliant villages were a little different. They did as they were told by the soldiers and bowed respectfully to the king even if their expressions betrayed them. Many of them had experienced the brutishness of the Romans, they may have shown some initial reluctance towards their invaders but, being the weaker of the colonies, found themselves pressed into shape. The older members bore scars, both physical and mental, from these first encounters with foreign forces. They would still sit and listen as I read. Some would sit in defiance, their faces stony and grave, but in the youth I saw a light that revealed my work would not be fruitless. Adlais did happen to have some influence. On the surface she appeared to be a sweet creature as she skipped and danced her way through the crowds with more energy and optimism than any adult could muster. She was flawless and, even at her young age, turned heads due to the deep pools of her eyes and soft blushed skin. When she first joined our party I tried to act as a mother figure; I was concerned that being taken from her family would have affected her in some way. However, she showed no interest in me and instead chose to hang onto Fagan's cape until he tired of her and swatted her aside. After she picked herself up without a tear, she would move onto Deruvian who would sweep her off her feet and dangle her upside down or swing her around until she laughed hysterically. She would then ride at the front of his saddle with him or, if he was walking, sit on his shoulders where she would snooze without a care in the world. It seemed as if she had already forgotten her mother and father. I wondered how I would have reacted if the situation had been reversed and I had been taken as a child. I wanted to believe I would have missed my mother terribly and would not have bowed to any false idols thrust upon me, but the more time I spent away from the bubble of the convent, the more shades of black and white I seemed to see.[31]

---

31. It is strange that I should've been poring over this chapter on the train to Cardiff. When I walked into the museum I was greeted by the curator, who had been expecting me due to a telegram from my friend at the British Library who had ignored my advice, and his little daughter, who hid behind his leg and gave me such a suspicious glare that for a second I thought Adlais had come to the present. She continued to give me a dirty look as I discussed the document with the curator until I was more focused on what she was up to than the grown-up talk I was supposed to be having. From what I could tell the curator was not at all pleased with the removal of the document from their archives. Despite its connection with the church, he believed it was of huge importance in learning how Wales and in fact the entirety of Great Britain was shaped to become what it is today. This is where I suggested we go somewhere quieter to discuss my findings. He took me into a small office and made me a cup of tea. I told him that I had seen the original document in Latin and that I was aware it had been in his care before it was taken from the library in Paris. I told him how pleased I was to find that it was as old as it claimed. I expected him to react to my knowledge of the original document, but he just nodded without interest, which prompted me to ask if he had read the original in full and whether he could answer some questions I had. He told me he had studied it in detail and then became still as if he mulled something over in his mind. While he did this the little girl spun around in a circle, fell on her bum due to the dizziness, and then looked daggers at me as if I had pushed her over. The silence became uncomfortable, so I asked him why he believed it to be such an important part of the history of Great Britain when the accuracy of the content could not be accounted for. I told him that at best it only really tells us the story of a Spanish fortune-teller of the medieval era. Here he looked at me in a worried fashion in an attempt, I think, to decide if I should be trusted. He must have decided I could because after this he took me deep into the heart of the museum's vaults where the dust lay thick on every surface and showed me something I had not expected to find. He opened a worn wooden chest with a rusted key and, with white-cotton-gloved hands, lifted out a scroll of ornate paper that looked as fragile as fallen leaves. Inside the trunk were several other scrolls, some almost skeletal in their thinness, but all looked as though they had been made around the same time. 'This,' he told me, 'is why I know the document is an important step in the knowledge of our history.'

So I now know that the original document had not been an original document at all. As far as the Church is aware it is in fact the only documentation of the events of Christianity entering Britain and Gueraula de Codines was much cleverer and more underhand than they know. The curator believed she had in fact found the scrolls, realised how important they were and how likely that they would be destroyed or hidden from general knowledge, and made up the story of her psychic channelling of Tavia to create a decoy document to pull the attention away from the real secret. It was a classic sleight of hand magic trick performed by a woman who outsmarted the Vatican and was still outsmarting the church today.

The curator has allowed me to read the scrolls and study them with the knowledge that I should not publish what I have found out or tell a soul. Though the curator of the entire museum, he says he's there to protect the façade that Gueraula de Codines had worked hard to build and to pass the responsibility to someone he trusts when he becomes old and needs someone to guard the secret after he dies. That person would be his daughter, he told me as he patted her on the head. Well she certainly already had the piercing and mistrustful glare of a guardian of great treasures.

From the small amount I managed to read it seems the original scrolls are in fact written by Fagan himself. Although Tavia had not written the original document she is mentioned as one of the people who travelled with him along with Deruvian although in the scrolls they are written as Faganus and Deruvianus and they travelled with a larger entourage who helped carry, cook, and gather supplies during the expedition. The writing in the scrolls is far more simple, and factual, in its information, without the flourishes and storytelling set down by Gueraula de Codines. In fact it is quite dull and formal in its details as it describes provisions and expenses incurred during their travel. Had I not been told what it was I would have read a little and probably stopped unless I had been an extremely keen scholar of Roman writing with nothing to do with my time.

I've decided to stay in the area for a while. I've found a quaint bed and breakfast in the close by coastal town of Penarth which is where I sit and write now. I've told the curator that I'll be back tomorrow to continue the study of the document. He was accommodating and seemed somewhat more relaxed when I left as if I had helped him to carry some of the weight of the secret that had been on his back for all these years.

Eight

At midday, Tabitha pulled herself out of bed and opened her curtains. The autumnal sun was gold and had filtered the sky to a bold blue. The house was silent but she could hear tyres on gravel: a geometric pattern of sound echoed through her skull. As she went downstairs there was a tinkle of a teaspoon against a mug and the squeak of a chair on linoleum. When she entered the kitchen her mum was sitting at the table, her mug next to the words 'AM I ADOPTED?' Tabitha couldn't remember when she'd carved the letters deep into the wood; the last week had flicked by like skipped chapters. Her mum pursed her lips when she saw her.

'Did we need the dramatics?' she said, with some worry but a cold surface to her voice.

'Well, isn't it?' said Tabitha. 'Dramatic, I mean?' She made herself a cup of tea, sat down opposite her mum, and sipped. Her mum's brow furrowed as her eyes latched onto the message.

'Honestly,' she said after a while, 'I thought you knew.'

'How would I know?' Tabitha asked. 'I was a baby.'

'You were three ... nearly four. I thought you would've been old enough to remember.'

'Three?' Tabitha said. 'Do you remember stuff from when you were three?'

'Yeah, that's why I thought you might remember. And it would've been a big deal for you.'

'But I didn't,' said Tabitha, 'maybe it wasn't as big a deal as you thought.'

She drank another mouthful of tea. After she'd figured things out, the memories of that time had come back – so fast and detailed that she thought some must have been false. She'd hoped her mum would tell her she was silly and she had not been adopted at all. She thought psychosis brought on by the heavy drinking would have been better. Her mum asked why only now Tabitha had suspected

101

she had been adopted. Tabitha told her that she had read something about an adoption that had triggered memories.

'So you do remember,' said her mum in an attempt to offload some guilt. Tabitha's eyes narrowed. 'Alright,' her mum admitted, 'I should've said something'. She got up and began to rummage through the china chicken on the Welsh dresser filled with bits of useless important things. After that she moved to a pottery jar that had once contained chutney but now acted as an overflow for the chicken. 'There it is,' she said, and then, 'here,' as she handed it to Tabitha. It was a key that, as her mum explained, her birth mother had insisted she keep safe for Tabitha. It was the only thing they asked for so she felt obliged to though it was rusty and she was given no detail of what it might open.

'I suppose this is some kind of symbolic bullshit my neglectful mother thought up in a drug-addled state,' Tabitha said as she took it and dropped it dismissively in front of her. Her mum sat down again and said she didn't know why she'd insisted on it and she wished she could tell her more about her birth parents but she couldn't. All she knew was they were addicts who had hit rock bottom. She wasn't even sure if they were still alive and she felt sorry for them because they had to give up their only child.

Tabitha tutted. 'At least now I know where I get these shitty genes from,' she said. 'Now I know where my life is headed I might as well do what the fuck I want.' Her mum sighed as Tabitha got up and went back upstairs, taking the key.

What followed over the next couple of months was a half-hearted attempt to keep on track but a lack of motivation. Most days she would turn up late to work in the church grounds and leave early. She would miss days, first one a week, then two, then she stayed home and slept late into the afternoon, when she would start to drink again. She would, more often than not, stay in to drink as she could make her money go further. After this had gone on for some time the church had a management meeting and decided to let Tabitha go. The decision had gone against the Reverend Geraint's thoughts. He was a soft, genuine, and charitable man at heart and had wanted to keep her in work and support her through difficult times. He had even gone to the house to speak to Tabitha's mum and, even after Tabitha had told him to fuck off through a drunken haze, listened to what had happened and tried to help.

It was a weekday afternoon. Her days had started to merge together, though it might have been a Thursday. Tabitha woke up and was coaxed from her bed by a scratched dry throat and a snarl in her stomach. She ate some cornflakes which became sludge before she got halfway through the bowl. She added another spoon of sugar and shovelled them in anyway. Her mum had already left for her shift and had scratched 'be good' into the tabletop. A coaster had been placed over the word 'ADOPTED' and left 'AM I' visible. In the fruit bowl in the middle of the table sat some browning bananas, a dry wrinkled lime which Tabitha had intended to make margaritas with, and the old key from her biological mother. Underneath it sat a twenty-pound note. She scrunched the key up together with the note and pushed it into her pocket.

Tabitha didn't want to go back to the old hangouts – they were in a different lifetime – and although The Nag's Head had not been her kind of pub it was the first that came to mind. She drank a couple of cans of lager from her bag on the bus on her way over and walked through the door with a gentle warmth that was built on foundations of the previous day's booze. As she entered she saw Alex sitting in the corner alone reading a book with his pipe lying unlit on the table. She was surprised to find that she felt slight excitement at seeing him there. After the initial shock about her adoption she'd gone into a bland emotional state that was only relieved by mild crossness now and again. After she'd bought two pints of ale she walked over and sat opposite him.

'You don't mind, do you?' she said as Alex looked up and his bottom lip quivered. His neck and shoulders tightened as he tried to stutter a reply that never manifested.

'Here,' she said as she passed over one of the pints she'd intended to drink herself, 'I bought you a drink.'

The gesture only broke the silence for a second as he thanked her softly in his throat and took a tentative sip. It took one more pint and a shot of Jägermeister for Alex to thaw and join in with a conversation that, up until that point, had been one-sided. Tabitha told him all she remembered of her birth parents and the adoption and memories of moving to the house she lived in now. Alex sat with a face that suggested he might be devoured at any moment. 'But I can't even believe it myself,' Tabitha said with a squeak at the end, and then she moved in closer to him and whispered, 'it's almost as if someone … or something … has set me up.'

'Well,' said Alex, cheeks now flushed, 'if we're going to go into the realms of paranoia, I might need an extra drink.'

There was a pause – fear in the air – worry that he might have said the wrong thing. Tabitha chuckled and every molecule in him breathed relief. Alex then got them both a drink before they headed outside so he could smoke his pipe.

'I know it sounds fucking nuts,' she said, 'but it's all come at a weird time in my life.' After she watched the smoke from the pipe rise into the crisp evening she said, 'I've been reading this book … well document kind of thing,' and then she told him some selective information which still felt like a betrayal, even while drunk. Alex sat and listened with interest because of his love of theology, as he told her, but also maybe for the freedom to study her face. He offered a few sensible suggestions, such as the nature of the document and the stressors in her life bringing what seemed like lost memories to the surface. He also gave examples in psychology when this would happen. He was much more clever and useful with his advice than any of her old friends would have been.

They then moved on to the treatment of her problems which, at Tabitha's suggestion, was shots of tequila and several more hours of drinking. Back inside, while Tabitha's fluid intake intensified, Alex began to nurse his pints for longer as his conversation became broken and his body swayed and wobbled on his seat. When time was called at the bar Tabitha prised him up and, through a fog, led him out the front door and into the cool of a moonless night. They sat on a bench on the periphery of the grounds of Llandaff Cathedral, which was a short stagger up the road. The cathedral was down the hill from them. A light shone from a window in the tower and lit the leaves of a nearby maple to create a cascade of deep red. The fresh air had invigorated the alcohol in their systems and Alex now slumped to one side and stared at the stars. Tabitha continued to chatter as he remained silent, but in time she stopped and looked up too.

'There's too much of it,' he said, 'in every way – direction – is too much.'

'I,' said Tabitha, pointing to herself, 'I too felt like that, you know, but then I was like, "who gives a shit".' She laughed as Alex frowned. Her arm found its way over his shoulders and then he began to laugh too. 'I mean … my birth mum abandoned me and all I got was this piece-of-shit key,' she reached into her pocket and showed it to him. 'She didn't give a shit, I don't give a shit, no one gives a shit … then you die.' She laughed again and pressed the key deep into the palm of Alex's hand. He studied it for a moment, his eyes squinting as he tried to focus.

'Looks … I seen this key … looks a bit like museum keys,' then his brow furrowed at his own statement and he started to giggle. 'Mmmuseumm keys!' he repeated as Tabitha joined in and gave his back a good slap.

'What the fuck are you on about?' she said, which caused the dialogue to move onto how much Tabitha swore. After half an hour on the bench Tabitha's mind started to clear and feel uncomfortable and then what followed was a to-and-fro of what to do next. Tabitha wanted to go into town to continue the night or go to the shop to buy a crate of beer and Alex struggled to hold a conversation but most of his suggestions involved home. Through her drunken lucidity, which was usually callous and cried for self-pacification, she saw a young man who looked afraid. 'Come on,' she said as she dragged him up by his arms, 'let's get you home.'

Tabitha suspected that Alex had never been as drunk before. Despite this he was like a homing pigeon and took her to the front of his house which he shared with others who had chosen the church as their vocation. She helped him with his keys which leapt and squirmed in his hands as he tried to control them, and then snuck him in through the door with fingers on lips and the odd shush when he hiccupped or sniggered. They made their way through the black and white tiled hallway and up the steep stairs to his room. Inside was a bed, a desk, and piles of books. It felt empty until Alex rolled in and slumped on the mattress and filled the space. Tabitha closed the door behind them and stood looking at him as he dozed off. He wasn't the sort of man she would go for – clothed like a man in his forties but with a young, scrubbed face. His hair was unstyled and his arms and legs were skinny despite his torso being round at the edges. She went over to the bed and curled up next to him and, even though he was semi-conscious, a hand came out and held hers. As she fell asleep, tears dripped down her cheeks.

She woke up a few hours later before the sun had come up. Alex had rolled to the furthest point of the bed from her, so she got up and left as quietly as she could. She wasn't sure if the boys in the house were allowed to have female visitors, let alone have them stay overnight in their single beds. She walked home through still neighbourhoods until more cars appeared on the road and the sun began to rise. Eventually she got back to her own house and saw that her mum's car was still not there. At least she would be able to get in without being noticed.

As she got into bed her phone vibrated. She thought she'd remembered most of the night but she didn't remember exchanging numbers with Alex. They must have though, because his name came up on the screen with the message. 'Hi Tabitha,' it said, 'I'm sorry for the trouble I caused, thank you for getting me home.' She smiled. The only apology text she had ever sent after a night out was to a friend she'd threatened to stab with a broken bottle after an argument about the origins of Redstripe lager. She texted him back, 'no trouble, speak soon.' As she got into bed she remembered the fear and guilt she felt with her hangovers when she started drinking as a teenager. She was beginning to drift off when the vibration of her phone on the floor woke her again. 'By the way, I still have your key. Sorry, I will get it back to you,' read Alex's text. She thought for a second before she knew what key he was talking about. When she realised her face went cold and her hair roots prickled. She hadn't thought it was important to her but now someone else had it she wanted it back immediately.

The next afternoon she caught the bus to Llandaff and knocked on Alex's door. Steven opened the door, the boy who had been with Alex the first time she met them at the pub. He was shorter than she was and he looked her up and down without a smile.

'Can I help?' he said.

'We met in the pub,' she said sharply. 'Is Alex in?'

'I don't know,' Steven said as he recoiled and stepped back from the doorframe.

'Well can you check?' she said, as she attempted some warmth that came across as sarcasm. He muttered something and nodded before he closed the door. A few moments later it reopened and Alex stood in front of her with his cheeks crimson and his eyes downcast. He apologised for Steven's manner and then apologised again for his own behaviour the night before and as she stepped towards him, to console and assure him that she wasn't upset in any way, his instinct moved him backwards.

'I just want the key back,' she said, feeling hurt at the broken bond they had built from the night before. The door was shut again as she waited. He said sorry again and as he handed her the key their fingers grazed together. He snapped his hand away as if he'd caught it on the flames of an open fire. Before he went back inside he found enough courage to lift his head and look at Tabitha's face. His gaze paused there a moment then stared at the floor again. He muttered his goodbyes and closed the door with a shaky hand. Tabitha went home and holed herself up in her room like a leper. She ran through the previous night and wondered if something else had happened that she'd forgotten about, something awful she'd said or done to upset Alex. In the end, she put it down to his inexperience with alcohol and women before she watched a film and dozed through the evening.

Winter fell fast that year. On bonfire night the air was thick with fog and the smell of gunpowder and, before midnight hit, the temperatures plummeted. By morning, the trees had shivered off the last of their leaves which lay hard with frost on the frozen ground. By the end of November Tabitha's mum had also started to grow cold at her daughter's idleness. She was sick of coming home to find her collapsed in front of the television as it boomed out programmes of no interest. Tabitha would do nothing around the house, not even clean her own bedroom, which had become a rat's nest of dirty washing and empty cans and bottles. There was no movement from Tabitha to find a job or even a hobby despite her mum cutting off pocket money. In fact, the discontinued money meant Tabitha never left the house at all and that was in some ways worse than her drinking.

Christmas was a month away and Tabitha's mum flitted around the house in a flurry of housework in preparation for the tree and decorations. She wanted to leave Tabitha's room dirty to teach her a lesson or prompt her to action or anything but she couldn't and so began to tidy. When Tabitha went to bed that night, after her mum had gone to work, she noticed the room felt bigger and somehow emptier though at first she was unsure why. She took a deep breath and felt her shoulders relax and as she lay down on fresh sheets and smelt the furniture polish realised her mum had cleaned. The books that Marguerite had given her had been taken from the bag and put up on her shelves. The document was placed on the end of her bed, complete with the stains and creases it had collected from being on the floor for so long. Tabitha picked it up and considered reading it before she put it down. After a minute she held it again and turned to the page she had last read. She then looked at the amount of pages that were left until the end. It wasn't many and the damage had already been done.

VIII

Faganus

A year elapsed and we had contained all friendly and compliant villages. As time passed, Lucius's attention to the cause began to wane. By the end of the initial period he stayed in the villa with Arthfael whilst we continued the mission. Hadrian had sent, at Lucius's request, an expert in wrestling and Lucius spent his time in nude combat with some weaker members of his staff. Due to an inexplicable attack of nostalgia, King Lucius desired to relive a distant and distorted memory of his youth. Arthfael was the first to point out that when Lucius was a boy he despised wrestling, but the king dismissed this and complained that Arthfael always deterred him from his dreams. Lucius was, in fact, a terrible wrestler. The expert Hadrian had sent was kind. He dismissed the king's failures in form as individual style and pitted him against the scrawniest of help who were pre-warned not to try hard. The expert forbade any bouts with Fagan and Deruvian, despite Lucius, after a few "successful" matches, being confident he could take them on and win. The expert was aware that Fagan and Deruvian were the kind of men who could not hold themselves back. There was a real chance one of them could accidentally snap the king's neck within the first move. The expert kept this from King Lucius and instead told him the two men would not be worth the bother. He placated Lucius by engaging with him in a gentle bout and even then, in a momentary lapse of concentration, almost broke Lucius's arm.

We returned one early autumn day to find a hideous intertwining of naked male bodies. In an instant of inspiration, Lucius had turned his opponent on his head and his opponent, requiring something to hold on to, had clutched the king's genitals. I gasped and covered my face, though this now felt like an affectation. The longer I stayed in Britannia with these men the more my sensibilities had numbed. Once they finished, the king of course being the victor, I expressed my displeasure at the display. I told them that a man of God, a man who had been baptised, should not participate in such a bloodthirsty and sinful pastime. As I spoke, Deruvian and Fagan took their clothes off and began to grapple. The expert stood in awe of their abilities and before long Lucius had begun to cheer from the side. I was left alone. I wanted to be angry, but it was difficult to deny the grace of their athleticism and the perfect creation of their bodies, a testament to the power of God. I am not afraid to admit there was still a dark part of my soul that would have liked to have stayed and watched, and a part that was convinced that if I had, I would not be a bad person. I ignored it and went to the Sacrarium to pray.

The men waited in the villa throughout autumn. Fagan had suggested they wait until the depths of winter before contact was made with non-compliant and hostile villages. He declared that by midwinter many of these villages would be at their weakest. The cold weather would eradicate many elders, as it so often did, and leave communities under less experienced leadership. At first the soldiers had shown reluctance towards Fagan's plan. The general explained to Fagan that the cold weakened his numbers as a lot of his men were from warmer parts of the world. Even soldiers who had been in Britannia for several years found the combination of damp and bitter temperatures too much to bear. The briefness of the days and lack of light also plunged some into an equal darkness of the mind. Between the previous December to February, five had died by their own hand. Fagan informed the general that his input was appreciated but stated with clarity that raids would still be carried out during the worst months. Although callous, Fagan would not send the soldiers to their deaths. He had enough practice in war to know that men were much more useful to him alive.

To remedy the weakness in the ranks, Fagan set up specific cold weather training. He banned the use of heating in the barracks on all days except Fridays. Each morning the soldiers would be forced to bathe in a nearby stream which sometimes had a layer of ice over its surface. They were required to stay in the water for at least ten minutes and the same ritual was repeated at night. After morning ablutions they marched naked until lunchtime. After the loss of a few toes in the first month, Fagan allowed shoes to be worn for the remainder of the programme. Some of the soldiers realised that, if they whipped one another's backs with stinging nettles, they could find some relief. When Fagan found out he banned this practice and threw the guilty parties, still entirely naked, into a nettle patch. As they scrambled to get out, they tore their skin to pieces on brambles that lay in wait amid the undergrowth.

The barracks had a man posted as a medic, but he was not compassionate and would not treat ailments that were not a threat to life or limb. If a man came to him with anything less, the medic would be catapulted into a fit of rage as he embarked upon a speech outlining the selfishness of their actions and the preciousness of his time. When I learnt of the soldiers' neglect, I began attending the barracks on Fridays when the soldiers were allowed to rest. Once there, I would treat their cuts, grazes, and chilblains with warm water and ointments. The soldiers were grateful for this and always polite and respectful. Sometimes I would look for the young man who had taken me to the safety of the grotto that day, but he never appeared. I liked the work, it gave me something to focus on and it reminded me of home. Every December at the convent, we would invite the needy inside, feed them, and wash their feet. I enjoyed doing this at the convent too. I met new people and the needy always seemed more interesting than the other nuns with whom I spent so much of my time. The poor came to me with the richest stories. They broke my heart with accounts of dead children, shocked me with the crimes of passion they had committed, and stirred me with their knowledge of the world and the seas. I was amazed by how people opened up when I performed these acts of kindness and the soldiers at the barracks were no different. I heard about their loved ones whom they had to leave behind, I heard about the homelands that some had been driven from due to Roman rule, and of the horrors they had seen on the battlefield. These insights made me feel as though I had part of my gift back. Their souls might not have communicated to me directly, but through their tales I could hear them speak.

It was on one of these Fridays that Fagan came to me. I was surprised, as something in me believed his body to be marble. As I finished with the last soldier that day he moved into the room without a sound and stood away from the fading light of the watery sun. The soldier left, and as Fagan did not move I started to pack up my things. Another man shuffled in with a candle as the room dimmed and I thanked him. When he had left, Fagan stepped forward with decisiveness and told me to look at his feet. There was no 'Would you mind?' or 'Please,' he just told me to look at his feet as he dropped onto the stool. I knelt beside him and began to unpack my lotions and cloths again. He waited for me to take his shoes off. His sullen face was unmoved as I peeled them away. I had seen his bare feet before, they were well-formed and strong, but the feet I liberated that day were unrecognisable. Every inch of skin on the tops were covered in chilblains and underneath were open raw blisters that covered the entire ball and heel. I asked him why he had not come to me sooner, to which he replied with his signature grunt. I spent a while washing them with great care. Although he appeared not to feel pain of any kind, it was clear he suffered some soreness otherwise he would not have come. I dried them with the softest hand I could muster and began to apply lotion. At one point I thought I saw him wince. A part of me had hoped he would speak freely as the others did but he chose not to say a word. Despite his best efforts his body gave some things away, and I knew he was uncomfortable. His legs and feet tensed as I came near and the veins of his hands stood out, and his silence was not the usual confident silence, there seemed to be an element of embarrassment. I opened the second bottle of ointment and poured a little on a cloth. As I reached forward and touched it to his foot, a sharp hand came out and grabbed my wrist. In shock I tried to pull away and he let go. 'That's enough,' he said as he stood up. I took a deep breath and told him to sit and let me wrap the bandages first. He sat again with some reluctance; I think he had reached an upper limit on how much compassion he was able to handle. As soon as I had tucked in the last end of gauze he was out of the seat and had disappeared into the darkness outside.

A month passed where nothing extraordinary happened. Fagan's interaction with me was the same as it had ever been, as expected. The man of marble remained stone. It was not until the troops were a week from their first exercise to a non-compliant village, that I received my first nocturnal visit. After that visit I woke in the morning in high spirits; I thought my gift had returned, so sure was I that it could not have been his actual physical form that had come but a projection of his deep desire to be close to another human. It was always unfathomably dark in my chamber, even on a lighter night when the moon was out in full, but I still knew it was Fagan. I stirred as he lay beside me; despite his size, he moved like a soft breeze when needed. There was little contact, only the back of his hand and his forehead touched me as he curled up on his side. I heard him grunt, but this time a grunt of contentment, as I drifted back to sleep. In the morning the bed was empty, which is what I had suspected, given that I thought the encounter was a vision.

The next night it happened again. This time I was not so fully asleep when he came, and I sensed his presence before he got in the bed. Without the cloak of sleepiness, it was now apparent that the actual man was in my chamber, not his soft longing-spirit but his hard, muscular, brutish body. As he got under the blanket my every fibre tensed and the hairs on my head prickled. Again, he curled up beside me, his hand and his head the only parts to touch. He let out a long sigh and I could smell his breath, meaty and sweet. His breath then lengthened and slowed as he drifted off. I wanted to shake him awake and tell him to get out, but I was afraid. I stayed awake for hours, in fear, and confusion at what these visits meant, what they would look like to God, and what part of Fagan needed this connection with another person. I thought I would not be able to sleep with him there but I must have because I woke up in an empty bed in the morning.

For the next three consecutive nights I had to endure his presence in the exact same way. By the sixth night I was exhausted, as I only slept a few hours before the sun rose. With tiredness, my horror and curiosity gave way to anger and annoyance. I stayed sitting up in bed, I did not want to sleep before he arrived. He slipped through the door again, as if he were the darkness in the room, and settled next to me. He did not speak or question why I was not lying down. He curled up in his normal manner and this time a gentle hand came over and rested on my abdomen, just below my navel. This new touch caught me off guard and for a moment I felt winded, as though he had punched my chest. I

113

managed to get myself together and said what I had rehearsed over and over before I blew the candle out that night.

'If you are looking for sins of the flesh, may I suggest the comfort women who call at the barracks on a Friday night.' I had seen them arrive as I packed my things after tending to the soldiers. They were young pretty girls, some seemed Roman, but many were local girls from the villages. I recognised several from our outings which proved that my sermons had fallen on deaf ears. I did not approve but there was little I could do and little other enjoyment in the soldiers' lives.

'Not as warm,' was all he grunted in reply before he went to sleep.

I was dazed for a moment. I expected more impact to my words but instead, when I heard his voice, it made the whole situation more real, and I felt frightened again. I managed to build up some courage and rolled slightly to the side to tip his hand off my belly. I managed to lie down before the hand skimmed back into its position. That night I was awake until he left just before dawn. As he got to the door, I heard him pause and whisper something. It sounded like 'Goodnight' or possibly 'Tonight.'

When I saw him during the day, after these peculiar encounters and before he went to the barracks or after he arrived back, his manner towards me was unchanged. The only exception was the morning after the seventh night. The visit began the same way the others had, Fagan moved into my room and I only knew of his presence when he began to climb into my bed. Like the night before, he rested his hand on my belly and sighed. It seemed that by this point I was resigned to my guest's whim. I was calmer this time and, maybe due to my fatigue, went into a light sleep soon after Fagan's breathing had changed. For the first time following the baptism I began to fall amongst wispy tendrils of dreams. I was still in my room, but it was somehow darker, and I could smell damp fur, raw meat, and blood. Claws pierced my abdomen, but instead of pain I felt heat and agitation like a scalding rash. The room was filled with a wintery forest, snow weighed down the pine branches and sap was heavy in the air. The heat from the claw spread through my body and I wanted to bury myself in the snow, but it seemed foolish to move the creature when it was not tearing me to pieces. As the burn moved to my throat, I began to choke, I could taste

114

iron, and then felt a weight on my ribcage. The dream began to fade from the room but the lump in my throat remained and the weight on my body. As my mind returned a real panic set in, when I realised that I still could not move. This time it was not some other-worldly demon like the night before the baptism, it was a body of flesh and blood. I could feel Fagan's hard naked body surrounding me as his arms pulled me closer. I tried to push him away, but he gripped so tightly. I could feel every scar on his rough skin, the welts on his back from numerous lashes, and his rough calloused hands catching on my tunic. I was disconcerted by the genitals pressed against my bare leg but my attention moved to his face which was pushed into my chest. I thought I could feel a dampness there as if he was weeping.

'You poor man,' I found myself whisper but not believe. That is how I stayed until morning, trapped in his tight embrace. He did not try to force himself upon me in any truly sinful way. I slept some but awoke again before dawn as he peeled himself away and left the room.

Later, I ate breakfast with Deruvian and Adlais. Fagan came in and sat down at the table opposite me. A faint smile was on Fagan's lips, something I had never seen. He held my gaze in a way he had not done before, and I hoped he would not do again. Through his pupils was a universe orchestrated by him. There was accumulative wisdom of the earth, the rocks, the water, and the savagery of the natural world, and they seemed to say, 'I can see you too.' I was so used to looking into the souls of others, that when someone looked into mine it felt strange and to have Fagan look was gut-wrenching. Deruvian asked Fagan to pass the water jug and the moment was broken. Adlais watched me throughout with indignation.[32]

---

32. Since I uncovered the scrolls, it hardly seems worth annotating this script anymore, although it is a good romp. I have continued to study the scrolls and I'm compiling my own private notes on them, which as I promised would be for my eyes only. With this in mind I suppose this document will have to remain private too. This has given me a great deal to think about. Since I was young my ambition has leant towards theology and the rich culture of humanity but now that has started to unravel. I was not brought up to be a cynic. My parents taught me that belief and faith was what kept us on the right path.

I went to the village of St. Fagans today. I suppose I wanted to see if there was a clue to the antihero in this story or a positive spin on this man's life. He was a saint after all. I did not find him there, just a small church, a post office, and a pub surrounded by quaint old cottages. The most notable part of the village was a large Elizabethan mansion, that they call a castle for some reason, which has been opened to the public within the last ten years or so along with the grounds. They have cleared much of the woodland in the grounds and are beginning to bring buildings from the rest of Wales to reconstruct there. It's supposed to be a new idea of an 'open air museum'. The head of the museum suggests this is a way of linking the past to the present instead of preserving 'the dead past under glass'. A commendable idea although I am beginning to wish the past had remained dead.

After I returned to Penarth, I took a walk along a cliff path. It was raining and the wind shook at my coat and tried to steal my hat. The sea was whipped up as it cracked against the stony beach and, as I looked out at the grey horizon and the jagged hard coastline smudged by the downpour, I felt a deep guilt. I thought of Isolde looking back across the choppy spikes of waves to Ireland, torn between faithfulness and love and filled with shame at her betrayal. A tension then built in me and I was compelled to jump but as tears began to stream down my face I experienced a sudden sense of release. I knew then that I would not return to France or finish my studies at the University. I would stay in this land, where my beliefs had collapsed, and make a life for myself. Now as I go to bed I realise that tomorrow will not only be a new day but a different life.

Nine

Tabitha was in the middle of a dream. She was at a party which had extended to the early hours of the morning despite it being a workday. She stepped over writhing, faceless bodies tangled in sexual acts as she tried to reach a phone, which rang constantly and she couldn't find. This went on for some time until she woke up to hear the ringing hadn't stopped. It was the house phone and it took her a few moments to comprehend what the sound was, as it very rarely rang. She lay there and ignored it until it stopped. If she ever picked up the house phone a voice, often recorded, told her it had been informed of an accident she had had that wasn't her fault. As she drifted off the image of a lawyer stood before her. In front of him was a man shot full of arrows. The lawyer then passed the man a key before the man fell and started to ring like a telephone on the floor. The sound seeped from his body like blood. Tabitha woke up again to find the noise of the phone echoed through the house a second time. After a while it ceased and the last chime reverberated through the brickwork. Tabitha lay still for a moment, the soft sheets warmed by her body, then willed herself to get up as it was almost midday. She ignored the phone a third time as she ate some cereal and when she went upstairs to brush her teeth she ignored it a fourth time because, even though she'd begun to feel curious about who it might be, she felt irritated by their persistence and felt it shouldn't be rewarded. When it rang a fifth time she happened to be walking past the phone, so she lifted it on the second ring and said, 'what?'

The other end was quiet for a few moments, and as rain lashed against her window, she could hear the same downpour at the other end.

'Is this Tabitha Edwards?' came an elderly woman's voice in reply.

'Yes, can I help you?'

'I have some bad news about your grandfather.'

'My grandfather?' Tabitha reeled a moment before she remembered both of her grandfathers were dead. 'I think you have the wrong Tabitha Edwards,' she said as she got ready to put the phone down. 'Both of my grandfathers are dead, one before I was even born.' She was about to say goodbye when the voice became hurried.

'Wait – I understand you're adopted? This is your birth grandfather, Tabitha.' There was a moment of silence again.

'Well in that case,' Tabitha said, 'I've never met him, so I suppose it doesn't really affect me.'

'I realise that might be true,' the woman replied. 'However, as he was a close friend of mine I was asked in his will to contact you and give you a letter from him. I don't know what it contains but I know he said it had something to do with a key. That was all he would say about the matter and was otherwise quite mysterious about it. Though he would tease me sometimes and give me a cock and bull story about conspiracy within the Vatican and throw in the illuminati or the Knights Templar now and again. He always had such a cheeky smile even when he was an old man,' she chuckled to herself.

'Okay, where is it?' said Tabitha as her heart smacked into the inside of her ribcage. Something clicked into place like the barrel of an old lock. She felt a flush of heat in her face as she tried to hold in excitement. It wasn't likely to be the original document that Marguerite had found. But maybe Marguerite had known more than she let on.

'Oh. Well,' the sudden interest took the woman by surprise, 'I can either come to you or you can come to the National Museum in Cardiff to fetch it. Are you close by?'

'I'll see you in an hour.' She put the phone down.

She was at the museum in less than an hour, her trainers and the bottom of her coat soaked, and went through the entrance followed by a flurry of wind, rain, and dead leaves. The elderly woman sat on a seat in the front hallway next to a sparsely decorated fir tree; her bony claw rested on top of a walking stick. As Tabitha walked over the woman rose to her feet, using the stick to balance, and held out her hand. Tabitha took hold and they exchanged a handshake while they introduced themselves. Her name was Myfanwy and she had a smile like warm towels and a voice round with a valleys accent. In each lengthened vowel Tabitha felt as though she'd met the woman somewhere before. As they walked into the museum, Myfanwy regaled Tabitha with stories about her birth grandfather and Tabitha felt a flutter in her stomach at the thought that Myfanwy might reveal herself to be her grandmother. It turned out that her grandfather's wife, Tabitha's actual grandmother, had died soon after she had given birth to Tabitha's mother. Her grandfather was heartbroken and had never remarried, despite being very good friends with Myfanwy for many decades. Aneurin, as Tabitha learned he was named, lost contact with his daughter after she married a man despite Aneurin's disapproval. It was another heartbreak for him, and he blamed himself. He felt that if he had approved of him maybe they wouldn't have lost contact and he could have helped her with her addiction. If he had done that maybe she wouldn't have died of the overdose. Myfanwy stopped here and apologised.

'I am so sorry,' she said as she turned to Tabitha, 'what an awful thing I've done,' there were tears in her eyes at the embarrassment. 'You wouldn't have known about your mother's death. That was incredibly insensitive and foolish.'

'Hey, don't worry about it,' said Tabitha.

'My dear,' Myfanwy said as her thin pencil line eyebrows rose to her forehead, 'are you sure?'

'Yeah, it's no problem, I didn't know her. I think I knew that she was dead somehow.'

Tabitha surprised herself with how much she didn't care. They went on until they reached the back of the museum, where Myfanwy entered a code into a door which led to all the archived artefacts. Here Myfanwy handed over the letter from her grandfather and told Tabitha that it was all the instruction she was given. She then told Tabitha that she would wait for her in the museum coffee shop and Tabitha was left alone.

The archives smelt of old paper and polish. Tabitha sat down at a large desk covered with tomes and opened the letter from her grandfather. It was written by hand in neat copperplate. It started 'My dearest Tabitha' and then went on to talk about her mother.

'I regret to tell you that your mother died a few years after you found new and more careful parents. She struggled for many years with drug addiction, and I cannot apologise enough for my absence at the time of her struggle. Had I known where she lived maybe I could have helped her but it was through my own pig-headedness that I lost contact with my beautiful child and allowed her to spiral to her death. I don't ask for your forgiveness but I hope you can still trust the words I write for you here.

'If your mother had retained some lucidity, and concern for her lineage she should have provided you with a key before she gave you up. I looked through her house after her death and couldn't find it, so I hope with all my heart that it is in your possession. I also hope that, although you may have been unaware of its importance, you have kept it safe. Though this might be hard to believe, the key has been passed through generations of our family since mediaeval times, or at least the key to a box that contains the real artefact that our ancestors have guarded for all this time. Whether this is the original box and key I can't tell you, but I can tell you that the artefact is indeed genuine. As a curator and a history lover it crossed my mind a couple of times that the document should be shared with the scholars of the world, especially as our world has changed so much and people have become more open minded. However, because of the trouble our ancestors have gone through to keep it secret, I knew I couldn't reveal its contents to the world.

'We don't know each other, Tabitha, but we share a blood line and I feel certain that the same wish to be a good custodian of this work will also be coursing through your veins. I'm sorry I didn't meet you whilst I was alive. Something held me back. I didn't want to disrupt your life but now, as I write this, I realise it was the fear of how you would receive me when you knew what had happened to your mother. I was a coward, and now you are having to hear this in a letter, and I won't be there to support you. I hope you can try to put this aside and think of the family members that came before me and do this for them.

'I wish you a full and wonderful life, Tabitha.

From your grandfather xxx.'

Inside the envelope with the letter was another smaller piece of paper with a number written in the same handwriting. Tabitha turned it over and frowned, looked around her, and came to the conclusion it must be the number of a shelf or something. Once she'd worked out that the letter in front of the number led her to a specific storage area, she could see the storage containers were numbered and then finding the number she had was straightforward. It wasn't long before she found the drawer with her number, tucked in a corner close to the floor surrounded by a soft smell of mould from the outside wall. There was a window next to her and a surge of rain splattered against the frosted glass as she pulled open her drawer. The metal ground against its runners as if it hadn't budged in years. Inside was a box – about half a metre square – made of metal and wood. She'd seen things on the telly, like *Antiques Road Show* where the experts would put white cotton gloves on their hands to protect a priceless object from the acids and filth of their body. Tabitha couldn't see any gloves and it seemed as though no one else had worn gloves either. The metal bits flaked with rust and the wood was compacted and worn, dark with grime and the grease from generations of fingers. She put the key into the lock and turned. There was a crunch as if the mechanism was full of dirt and the key jammed. She tried to turn some more but it felt as though it would break. She stopped a second to think. She could hear her blood as it whooshed in her hot ears. Unable to wait any longer she pressed down on the lid of the box and wiggled the key, with care at first then with vigour. There was a click in the lock barrel and the top opened.

A smell of pine filled the air and an icy draft accumulated around floor level. Tabitha shivered but didn't take note. She plunged her hand into the unlined box and took out one of two scrolls of old paper; it was soft like fabric and cold to the touch. She unrolled the end and took a peek. She had expected to find Latin and that is what it appeared to be, but it was disappointing. She hoped there would be illustrations or at least great curly colourful letters at the start of each paragraph and something to confirm what it was. She unrolled more but found the same blocks of writing in all the same colour inks. She sighed, rolled the paper back up, and as she placed it in the box had a sense that someone had walked in and was standing behind her. There was a creak on the floor, and she turned with an expectation she would see a museum staff member or Myfanwy but was faced with an empty room. At first this didn't shock or scare her – old buildings were often creaky and she had drunk too much on several occasions and thought people were around her when they were not. It was when she clicked the lock shut again, and as she did so felt some pressure on her shoulder, that she became nervous. She looked again to confirm no one was there and saw shadows around the shelves softening the solid forms of the books and artefacts. The walls and floors wavered and shimmered like light on water. She took a deep breath. It could be an LSD flashback, she thought, but as she moved to lie down a black shape lunged in front of her face. Surprised, she squealed and pressed herself against the floor. A few moments later she opened her eyes, dizzy and disorientated. The key to the box was on the floor and the lid was still open. She must have fainted before she'd locked it. She might have stood up too quickly and passed out through low blood sugar. Breakfast seemed like a long time ago now. As she closed the box and put it away in the drawer she could smell pine again. This time the scent was strong and made her feel sick as she stood up and wobbled.

Tabitha didn't meet Myfanwy in the coffee shop when she'd finished. She left the museum and went back home. Along with the faintness that followed her was joined a deep fatigue and she nodded off on the bus, only waking the stop after hers. She walked back to the house and despite being less than a quarter of a mile it added to her tiredness. Her mum was home eating lunch at the table when Tabitha came in through the front door. She looked up at Tabitha, concerned.

'Are you feeling okay?' she said.

'Just a bit washed out,' she replied as she filled a glass up at the tap. She took a sip and groaned.

'Where were you?'

'In town at the museum,' she said, and she dragged her feet back out of the kitchen.

'Museum?' her mum called after her. 'You must be poorly.'

Tabitha hauled herself upstairs and lay on the bed. She hoped she wasn't going to be ill over Christmas. She fell asleep fast and when she woke, later that afternoon, she felt a bit better. She went downstairs and found her mum putting up the Christmas decorations. Though it was only the two of them, and they would rarely have visitors, Tabitha's mum would always put up a tree and decorate. They used to have a real Christmas tree which they chose at a farm just outside Cardiff. The ritual would make her feel Christmassy and with a trip to see Father Christmas, usually on the same week, would mark the start of their festive period. Tabitha loved the woody scent as they drove back home. It felt as though she was sitting in a forest. Sometimes the tree was a bit too big and branches would engulf her in her car seat. She would sit with a grin on her face and watch the tiny insects and spiders crawl from branch to branch. When Tabitha became a teenager her mum bought a plastic tree. By this age Tabitha was out more with her friends and wasn't interested in going to the farm and picking out a tree. It also meant that her mum didn't have to spend all her time off work hoovering needles from the carpet and the furniture and from everywhere else.

It had been several years since Tabitha had helped with the decorations and she joined her mum to erect the tree and bend its wire branches out to make it seem more realistic. She saw her mum smile.

'I didn't even think you liked Christmas anymore,' she said to Tabitha.

'No ... I like it,' she said and fell silent as they hung the baubles and wound round the tinsel and fairy lights. Being taller than her mum, Tabitha could put their Christmas angel on the tree without standing on a chair. The angel had been put on the top of the tree for as long as Tabitha could remember. She was made of plastic, her head was like a small doll's head, and her body was a clear cone decorated in lace. Her wings were long gone – Tabitha couldn't remember what they had been like – and her short blonde hair was a matted mess with a gold halo stuck on. She had makeup on her eyes like a sixties Bond girl and had a calculated slyness on her lips. They turned on the lights and stood back to admire the work. It wouldn't be a window display for John Lewis but it was pretty and brightened the room. She'd always hated how the house looked after all the decorations were taken down on Twelfth Night. It added to the faded bleakness of January and every year she was sure she wouldn't get used to the bareness. But by the time a week had passed it was as if Christmas had never happened.

Afterwards they put up garlands and strings along the wall to hang up the cards. Tabitha's mum was still traditional with cards. She would spend hours with a pile of charity Christmas cards and her address book, writing one for everyone she knew and had ever known, regardless of whether they had returned one the year before. She stuck a stamp on each and posted them the same day. She would also write one for every person she looked after in the care homes she worked in and every colleague she worked with, even if she wasn't keen on them. Tabitha, on the other hand, hadn't written a card since school. When they finished with the rest of the decorations, Tabitha's mum made them a cup of tea and warmed up some mince pies. Outside the rain had cleared and the temperature was falling.

'Maybe we'll have a white Christmas this year,' said Tabitha's mum. She said it every December.

All afternoon Tabitha had wanted to tell her mum about the key and the box and the museum – it had been the reason she had started helping with the tree – but the time didn't seem right. There were a couple of moments when she was about to speak when her mum would say something like, 'how does that look?' or 'what do you think of that?' which was like a mute button. She then thought she would tell her afterwards but had enjoyed the afternoon more than expected and somehow it seemed as if the news could spoil the serenity, so she kept quiet. They watched old films on the TV and later ordered a Chinese takeaway which they ate with chopsticks they kept in the cutlery drawer. Later they went to bed at the same time and when Tabitha's mum came out of the bathroom she said goodnight and pulled Tabitha's bedroom door to in the same way she had when Tabitha was a little girl. Tabitha went to sleep faster than she had for a long time without the assistance of alcohol.

It wasn't until midnight had passed that Tabitha woke up feeling cold. She pulled the duvet up over her shoulders and nose and shivered as she curled into a ball. It didn't seem to help. The duvet itself seemed frozen and the smell of the Christmas tree seeped up the stairs and into her bedroom. There was another smell too, something musty and fungal with a hint of sulphur, like a wet dog. After this she drifted off again but woke an hour later when she felt a weight on her feet. This time she was more awake and wondered how she could smell pine when the tree was synthetic. She looked to the bottom of the bed and found nothing. She lay back down and fell asleep again. The next time she stirred was close to dawn. She was cold again but this time it was concentrated at her midriff and it was heavy as if there was an arm wrapped around her. The weight made her feel short of breath and she wondered if this was the resurgence of how she'd felt in the museum the previous day. She put a tentative hand to her stomach and on finding the form of an arm there jumped and sat up, throwing snow away from her as she surfaced into an ice-misted woodland. The jolt woke her fully – the bed was back, and her heart thumped audibly into the darkness of her room. She lay down and let out a heavy breath. Afterwards her mind fluttered over the events of the past year and the most recent encounters with St. Fagan. She waited in bed until the sun came up and then went downstairs for breakfast. Despite the early wake-up she felt well rested and cemented in her head what she would do that day. She only knew one person who could read Latin, so it would seem the first item on her list would be to visit Alex and try to repair the broken relationship. She knew this wouldn't be easy as she didn't really know why it had broken in the first place.

Ten

Predictably it was the gatekeeper, Steven, who opened the door. His face was a familiar picture of suspicion, bushy unibrow heavy over small sharp eyes.

'Is Alex here?' she said with tenderness and a smile that most normal men couldn't resist. For a moment he didn't speak. He didn't want to tell her Alex's whereabouts but his moral objection to lying won out.

'Yes … but I don't think he will want to see you.' Even a white lie seemed beyond his capabilities. He stood for a moment longer, then began to close the door. Tabitha put a hand on the edge to stop him. He was quite small so this wasn't difficult.

'Well, could you ask?' she said as her temper rose. 'Tell him it *was* a museum key.' There was another silence, though this time she held Steven's gaze until he looked down, shoulders hunched.

'Okay,' he said, and tried to close the door again, but this time the toe of Tabitha's shoe was wedged in the way. He slunk into the dim hallway until his footfall was replaced by muffled voices to and fro. This continued for a few minutes before the volume increased and Tabitha heard Alex's voice say, 'well it's not up to you, Steven,' as he moved into view. He spotted Tabitha as he peered through the gloom and jumped. She gave a friendly wave and his tentative palm raised in reply. He came out and shut the door behind him. There was some of the same distrust in his face but his body also shook with excitement as he glanced at her hands for the key or a clue to her visit.

They stepped off the bus into another downpour of rain and walked across the park to the national museum. It hadn't taken any persuasion to get Alex to make the trip. As soon as she told him about the Latin scrolls sequestered in a secret box under lock and key, a key that only her ancestors had possessed over decades, she could barely keep up with him on the way to the bus stop. She told him she thought the document she had was a decoy for the scrolls that were original Roman text. Alex was doubtful but she knew he couldn't ignore the possibility that the story was true and he stood to discover history so tangible it rewrote the beliefs of a generation. They were allowed access to the back of the museum. The people who worked there were aware of the secret box kept in storage and the key that had passed through the hands of the family of curators through the years. It was something of a legend amongst them and was often discussed with great enthusiasm during orientation of new staff members. Alex followed close behind, his shoes clipping the back of Tabitha's heels. It wasn't until they got to the damp corner with rain lashing against the frosted glass window that Alex stopped short. He crossed his arms over his chest as if cold and took a couple of steps backwards.

'I – I – I,' he stammered, 'I think I've changed my mind.' He began to turn but stopped. 'Do you smell that?' he said.

'What?' said Tabitha.

'It smells woody ... like pine trees or something.'

'Yeah, I smelt it before. I think it might be the box.' She motioned to the flaky relic she'd fished from the metal drawer.

'No, it smells fresh.'

'Dunno,' Tabitha said and shrugged. 'Maybe it's some automatic air freshener or they have a Christmas tree in the next room. Who cares?' She took out the key and Alex made a sharp movement towards her as he glanced over his shoulder.

'Don't bother to open it,' he said with slight panic. 'I probably won't be able to read it anyway.'

'You'll be fine,' she said with a frown. 'Besides we're here now, you might as well at least have a look.' As she crouched down to press on the lid and wriggled the key, Alex sat on his haunches too and pushed himself against her shoulder as his eyes searched the room. She opened the lid and turned her head to look at him. Small beads of sweat sprang from his now pale and waxy nose and brow. He wobbled and clung to her arm as he almost toppled backwards.

'Are you feeling okay?' she said. He shook his head in reply.

'Can we go?' he asked as he stood up on shaky legs. Tabitha

nodded and when Alex turned to leave, she put the scrolls in her bag. She locked the box and put it back in the drawer.

Outside Alex's colour returned and he apologised as they returned to the bus stop and sheltered from the rain. He couldn't tell Tabitha what was wrong but he said he'd felt a sudden heaviness on his body. Tabitha told him that she felt similar the day before and concluded that there must be something going around. Once they were on the bus she told him he could still read the scrolls as she unzipped her bag and showed him inside. The expression on Alex's face reminded Tabitha of a victim at the end of a slasher film, after they have escaped the fiend only to find them still alive and in pursuit.

By the time they had returned to Alex's house he'd calmed and appeared well again. His interest returned and they went into the small dining room to open them and see if he could make any initial translations.

'You know, these scrolls are extremely old,' he said, as Tabitha pulled them from her bag. 'Your ancestors would be turning in their graves if they saw you shove them into your bag like your homework,' he gave a smile.

'As if I ever did homework,' she said and laughed. Alex laughed too as he rummaged in the drawer of an old sideboard.

'Ah ha!' he said as he pulled out a pair of thin white cotton gloves. 'I knew we had some here somewhere.'

'What the fuck?' said Tabitha. 'Who has museum gloves in their house?'

'A nerd who likes to collect historical documents, that's who,' he said and winked in a bold move that surprised Tabitha. He put on the gloves and gently began to unroll the paper on the table. 'Well, it seems genuine,' Alex said, 'and I think you're in luck, the turn of phrase is a little odd at times but I can read it alright. And here is your man – Fagan – mentioned right at the start.'

'Great,' Tabitha said as cool as she could muster.

'Don't get too excited, it's pretty dull stuff. Just itineraries and inventories to start with.' He unrolled it further. 'There seems to be some more description of the journey itself here but it's dry.'

'Figures,' said Tabitha, as she slumped down on a rickety dining chair and sighed as it creaked beneath her.

'It still might hold some interesting history,' Alex said, as Tabitha groaned. 'There has to be something of interest in here. It has been kept under lock and key. Don't despair, pretty one.' Now Alex looked directly at Tabitha and smiled in a way she hadn't seen him smile before. It was a large toothy grin with a mischievous glint. 'Leave it with me for the rest of today and tonight and I'll work through as much as I can before I see you again tomorrow.'

Though she was unsure whether to leave the scrolls, there was a shift in Alex that took her off guard. Instead of voicing reservations she found herself ushered to the door and sent home with a kiss on the cheek, which burned a confused path towards her brain and nested there for the rest of the day. She went home and ate dinner with her mum. When she didn't speak her mum asked if she was okay. Tabitha muttered a 'Yes,' and carried on eating. She went to bed that night with the key under her pillow. Despite the box now being empty, she gripped onto it with a hand beneath her head and woke the next day with its imprint deep into her palm.

The next day she knocked on Alex's door and it opened within seconds to reveal a smiling face. Alex pulled her in, her feet clipping the threshold. He took her to his bedroom where his curtains were half closed and his bed a tousled mess. He shut the door behind them. The scroll was dog-eared and unfurled across the carpet. As he moved towards it, he kicked over a glass of water which began to seep onto the paper. Alex mopped at it aggressively with a dirty T-shirt while he spoke in rushed and high-pitched tones about what he'd read. He'd given up on the cotton gloves and now manhandled it with fingers slick with natural skin oils. As he explained the contents to her, he rolled the edges in and out with abandon, pointing here and there at the text as if it would help her to understand.

'So you see,' he said, 'this explains the mystery of how Christianity came to be in Britain in the first place.'

'So why was it kept so secret?' said Tabitha as she straightened out the duvet and sat down on the edge of Alex's bed.

'Well … I suppose it could've been considered unpalatable to a more modern reader. There are lists of villages etc. that were forced to conform and – even though it doesn't go into gory details – it is explicit on the numbers of people who were killed and oppressed to make this happen.' Alex smiled. It was a warm smile and his head tilted to the side as if a pleasant thought had entered his head. Tabitha shifted on her bum and cleared her throat. She would have preferred to be back home. There was a tension in the room that reminded her of life with Tyler. 'Of course,' he continued, 'if we take into account your document, it might actually have been hidden for fear that the church would destroy it. It's incriminating evidence, not only about the brutality Christianity brought to the country but also the fact that it was fundamentally started by a woman. But if it's kept under lock and key forever it kind of has the same effect. Don't you think?'

'This … this doesn't bother you at all?' was all Tabitha could reply as Alex came to sit next to her. He shook his head.

'I think it's exhilarating,' he said. 'It's ancient history, right? The world's changed and people understand these were different times. Maybe it's time the world knew about this.' Alex put a light hand on Tabitha's knee, where she left it due to pure shock at the action. 'To let everyone know what these men – and woman – accomplished.'

He grinned that grin again – the one that had astonished her the previous day. Had he done this when they first made friends she would've been fine but there was a change in him that seemed uncharacteristic and almost unreal. This transformation seeped through his pores and even into his expression. It reminded her of an impressionist on a TV reality talent show whose whole face seemed to alter as he mimicked the prime minister, as though he became a different person through imitating the habits and speech patterns of someone else. The shy, clever Alex had vanished and the faked confidence and bravado was replaced by the conviction of a heavyweight champion. Tabitha stood up with a sudden jerk and caused the hand to fall back onto Alex's own lap. When she looked back at him she saw a moment of hurt, proof that the Alex she knew was actually in there still. There came a stifled 'Sorry' from him and he settled. Tabitha was pleased when he suggested they go downstairs to discuss the scroll some more. She agreed and bolted from the room.

Steven sat watching television in the living room. He glanced at Tabitha and gave a grave nod. His general look of suspicion had thankfully left. Alex flumped onto the couch next to Steven while she perched on the edge of a tartan armchair. Alex gave a heavy exhale and repeated, 'yes, the world's become a different place.' Steven nodded once more, as if he'd been privy to the previous conversation though his wide eyes remained set on the screen as the channel replayed *It's a Wonderful Life* for at least the fourth time that year. His pupils darted here and there as they followed the grey scale figures on screen.

'I love this film,' said Alex, 'despite its inaccuracies.'

Tabitha felt more at ease and sat back to watch too. Tightness had built in her shoulders, risen up her neck, and had begun to twist her scalp into a headache. The boys sat silent, mesmerised by the story, only the twitch of an odd half reaction flitting across their hypnotised faces from time to time. The room was chilly and by the time the film was in its final scene Tabitha's skin had raised into goosepimples. She shivered and brought her jumper sleeves over her hands and pulled her arms around her chest. She wanted to leave but lethargy kept her pinned to the chair. When the credits rolled she thought about the warmth of her own home and managed to struggle against the feeling and get to her feet.

'I've got to get home,' she said, her voice quiet and broken.

'I'll see you tomorrow,' said Alex as he made a lunge for Steven and got his arm into a lock and forced his hand into a peculiar wave goodbye. This sudden attack was then transformed into a sharp hard movement from Steven that ended with Alex in headlock as the two then rolled off the couch and began a full grappling session. Tabitha backed away and attempted a final, 'okay, see you,' before she turned and made her exit from the house.

On the bus home she sat above a heater and, as her flesh began to return to the temperature of a living person, her mind tried to make sense of what had happened. The boys had been out of character.

Or had they been out of character? She didn't know them well enough to recognise their full characters but when she'd met them before they hadn't seemed like that. They were training to become vicars, it didn't seem normal that they should grapple with one another on the floor or come onto her. But maybe they were *normal* men after all. They did seem out of the ordinary, though, or perhaps she was thinking too much about everything at the moment. This year had been tough; it was better to keep control of her imagination. She looked out at the drizzle and tried to focus on the sensation of the movement of the wheels and the reality of life at that particular moment. As she did so the events of the day floated about like the dust of a dream after awaking. This made her feel a moment of panic as she lost her grip on what was real and what wasn't. She practised some breathing exercises. She had been taught them during the compulsory anger management classes she'd done with a councillor at school after a few fights and the first run-ins she had with the police. It helped enough to get her home without a full meltdown in public.

When Tabitha stepped into her own home the knots in her shoulders dissipated. Her mum sat on the couch with a blanket and a book open upside-down on the arm. The lights on the tree cast a soft glow as a gentle snore rose from her mum's throat. Tabitha curled up beside her with her head on her mum's lap. Her mum woke up, blinked, and put a hand on her daughter's head. 'Is everything okay, sweetie?' she croaked. Tabitha nodded and closed her eyes.

She didn't feel like going to bed that night. Her room felt colder than usual, which her mum put down to having the door closed all day and the radiator in there needing to be bled. Her mum came in after she brushed her teeth and tucked her in, something she hadn't done for at least ten years. She stroked Tabitha's hair back off her face and kissed her forehead.

'Everything will sort itself out,' she said. 'Let's just have a nice Christmas together.' Then as she left the room, 'goodnight, sweetie.'

Tabitha gave her reply of goodnight but after her mum left the room she sat up and turned on her bedside light. She pulled the document from the drawer of her bedside table. She had a faint sense of Marguerite being nearby. Every cell in Tabitha's body told her to forget all about it; to forget the rest of the document, leave the scroll with Alex, and never go back. Her fear of missing out pushed her forwards. There was a compulsion to reach a conclusion of sorts, though she doubted if there was a conclusion to reach at all. Marguerite would have helped her through it; Marguerite somehow made the ground beneath Tabitha more solid and real than it had ever been before. Marguerite would have at least wanted Tabitha to finish reading the document. If she'd not wanted that why would she have left it for her?

IX
Vigils

The next three months were spent beneath Adlais's indignation. Fagan and Deruvian left for the barracks after breakfast to begin operations on the resistant villages. During this period we heard little of what happened in the field. We were only informed of successful outcomes. A soldier would return, one of their best riders, and notify the king of each placated settlement. When the first messages of victory reached the villa, I offered my services in bringing the word of God to the newly compliant natives. I was told my assistance would not be required and when I questioned, I was ignored. I was not sure who pursued the original mission plan, the king certainly did not. The wrestling expert announced one day that there was nothing more he could teach Lucius and went home with whatever patience he had left. The king then decided he would begin studies in ludus latrunculorum. As with wrestling, Hadrian sent Lucius a skilled adept to instruct, and as with wrestling Lucius learned slowly. He and Arthfael would sit, bent over a board for most of the day whilst the teacher gave Lucius tuition. Despite this Arthfael would still win most of the time and the teacher would get very cross because Lucius would not listen. Eventually, Lucius got tired of being scolded and sent the teacher away. After which Lucius and Arthfael would sit and play alone, Arthfael telling Lucius where to place the counters until he won. Lucius played Adlais once and lost.

I was put in charge of Adlais whilst the men were gone. She was furious that they did not take her with them. I tried to explain the dangers of the trip, but she would not listen, she would not even look at me when I spoke. At one time I thought I could take her to the Sacrarium, and we would pray together, and I could teach her to be a good Christian, but most of the time I could not even find her when it was bedtime. She would scamper and hide from me for hours in the villa and the grounds until eventually one of the servants would tip me off that she was hiding in the pantry, or the grotto, or the kitchen staff would have her backed into a corner like a rat. Then just like a rat, she would bite, scratch, and squeal as I grabbed her and took her to her chamber. She would spit at me and curse me in her native tongue as I tried to dress her for bed. As soon as she was put down to sleep she would get up again and escape into the dark of the corridors.

In the morning I would go to her room to wake and dress her. Each day I would hope her feelings towards me would have changed. I did not know what I had done to deserve such disdain. Sometimes her bed would be empty and I would have to scour the villa for her to ensure she would get breakfast. On a few occasions I found her outside, naked, filthy, and eating a rabbit she had caught or some berries she had found. She would shout and run off inside. Taking her to bathe and clean herself were out of the question. The only time I had got close resulted in a black eye for me and a split lip for her as she dashed to the door, slipped on the wet floor, and hit her face on the edge of the stone step.

If she was in a room and I walked in she would get up and leave, her face a picture of pugnaciousness. I followed her from room to room, suggested activities we could do together, games we could play, I would attempt to bargain with her, and bribe her with treats and lax rules. Nothing worked, and eventually I allowed her to get on with whatever most pleased whilst I kept a weather eye from a distance.

After a month of this disrespect, with her behaviour only worsening, I gave up. I had wanted to do her a favour, to be a mother for her, to be someone who would give her care and affection. However, it became clear I could not force my attention on her. Everything I tried made her miserable. I spoke to the servants, and they often informed me with regret that Adlais was happier when I was not around. They also told me that she had taken a shine to one of the older women who worked in the kitchen. The woman would give her scraps of food when she was good and smack her quite hard with a large wooden spoon when she misbehaved. I did not feel it was in me to hit the girl, it seemed she disliked me enough without me beating her, and through my childhood I had dreamed of a time when I had a body unblemished by cuts and bruises. On further investigation, despite the odd corrective clout, the cook seemed good with Adlais. I asked if she could put her to bed at the end of her day and get her up in the morning. She was not pleased with this as it added to her already long and dismal day, but she agreed, and I was free of Adlais. At first, the same thing happened when I walked into a room, but as the weeks passed she would stay and ignore me rather than leave. This was about the best it got. She never warmed to me, but her hatred faded. She played with the king on occasion, and she enjoyed time with Arthfael, who did not seem to want to play but was rather good with her nevertheless.

With Adlais dealt with, I had my time back and I decided to fill that time with God. I had not lost faith or love in God, but my focus had drifted and my concentration had waned. I felt I had to ask for much forgiveness.[33] Forgiveness for not keeping God at the centre of my life as I had done for so many years at the convent. I also wanted to ask forgiveness for those nights Fagan had entered my bed, but each time I thought about it the blood ran from my head and I became dizzy. When I tried to remember, it felt as though I stood on the edge of a cliff-face and, if I recalled the visits fully, it would be like hurling myself off. I knew I had done something awful, but the act of bringing it to mind seemed a sin in itself. It was clear in the scriptures that sin could be forgiven with repentance but I felt somehow that this did not apply to me. Maybe it only applied to men, or to sins that were listed or described. I could not place what my sin was, I could not draw it from a

---

33. I walked past the Church during this morning's walk. I had no intention of going in but I wonder why I'd decided to walk past on a Sunday morning at the exact time they would start the service. A force of habit I suppose. The vicar smiled at me and I was drawn in. The hymns seemed to clear my mind and for the time I was at the service, I was happy again. Happy to be told of the wonders of Christ and the good we can do in the world as individuals. My spirit was entirely taken in and cleansed until I came home and picked this up again. I question my resolve when I can so easily be swayed one way or the other by outside influences. I'd always thought of myself as a strong person but now I wonder if that thought process had been the very thing that made me weak. Maybe I'd be the confident sap who would be taken on stage by a hypnotist and made to cluck and peck at the ground like a chicken.

list or give it a name, all I knew was that I had sinned, it was inside me, a dark alcove where Fagan's slight smile glinted from the gloom. I knew the only way to deal with my sins was to go back to basics.[34] I began to organise my day to reflect that of the convent, my main focus on the spirit with a balance of physical work to help the flesh. I was early to rise and early to bed, and I kept myself apart from the rest of the household. It began to feel natural, as if I was home.

The convent, however, had not always felt like home. When I first moved there it was difficult to adapt to the rigour of the schedule laid out by Mother Superior. We would rise in the morning, at four o'clock, to the sounds of the chapel bell. By four-fifty we were in the chapel ready to begin our Liturgy of Hours. These started with the Vigils, which were followed by a reading of the scriptures. We would then meditate on what we had read and then pray. By six forty-five we embarked upon the fixed prayers of the Lauds, followed by Holy Mass, followed by the fixed prayers of Terce. After this we had breakfast which we ate in complete silence. After rising at four in the morning, in some ways this silence was welcomed, but was also impractical and frustrating at times when you needed someone to pass more bread or water and each grey face stared at the table in front of them. Waving arms about was not acceptable as I quickly found out.

This silence was also extended to noon dinner, although here one nun would read aloud from the scriptures or from an important letter or writings sent to us from Rome. Between breakfast and noon dinner we were expected to work in the convent, cleaning, gardening, or cooking. This work always felt like a welcome break from the intensity of spiritual work. I especially liked working in the garden because it gave a sense of space and distance from the other women. I often felt a stronger connection to God in the garden than I did in the chapel. I would sometimes whisper to the birds who came to eat the creatures I unearthed as I worked. We would then all be called in to the prayers of Sext before our food was served. After our midday meal we would work again, which was preceded by prayers of that hour, until Vespers at five

---

34. I'm beginning to admire her strength of character and single-mindedress, however fictional she might be!

in the evening. Supper was at six and also eaten in silence. After supper, many convents would allow some personal, if controlled, recreation. Our Mother Superior disagreed with this practice and instead we were made to kneel in private meditation until our night prayer at seven-thirty. During this time, we were not allowed to stand up or move at any point. Towards the end of this exercise it was difficult to think of anything other than the fire that grew in your legs and knees. It was not uncommon for nuns to injure themselves afterwards as they tried to stand, only to find their legs entirely not their own anymore. One particular nun lost her two front teeth as she rose suddenly at the request of Mother Superior and landed squarely on her face on the stone-slabbed floor. Another tore the ligaments at the back of her legs with a mighty pop and was unable to walk without sticks thereafter. Following night prayers we kept a strict silence again, which did not need to be enforced due to exhaustion. We would then sleep, and the process would be repeated the next day. This was our basic schedule that would be altered slightly for the days of the saints and important dates in the calendar like Easter and Christmas.

Despite being surrounded by other women, life in the monastery was lonely. The enforced silences made it extremely difficult to connect with anyone. The only person a nun would usually talk to was Mother Superior, and even then she would talk whilst you said, 'Yes Reverend Mother,' or 'No Reverend Mother.' I stood in front of Mother Superior about six months after my arrival when my gift had been noticed. I had found the adjustment to convent lifestyle very difficult and I had struggled to wake that morning. As I made my way to the chapel my body was filled with an ache that travelled through my veins into every part of my frame. My mind slipped from my control and started to conjure ways of escape, running away, committing an unforgivable sin that led to my expulsion, death by my own hand. But as I sat and listened to the Psalms during the Vigils, I was gripped by something. I felt a jolt down each limb with a pain so severe I yelped aloud. The sisters beside me turned to look but the scriptures continued to be read out. At this point I was thrown into a pure white light, lost in a great abyss where all time had arrested. There was no sense of up, down, left, or right. I was afraid so I began to crawl to try to find some perception of existence but the further I crawled the more I found nothing. I breathed hard and covered my face and when I took my hands away everything had fallen into blackness. It was a blackness that had no edge, no shadows, it was infinite. I then heard a voice. At the sound of it I wept as I knew it could help me find a way out of the emptiness. The voice told me of the importance of my existence. It told me that I would make a difference. I had experienced the gift before, outside of the convent, but it had not been as all-consuming, and I had not realised the experiences had been connected to God's work. When I returned to the chapel I was lying on the floor. The Psalms were still being read but a nun was kneeling beside me holding down my arms. The other nuns looked on, aghast. I only got snippets of what had happened in the chapel that day. Some of the nuns spoke of it in hushed tones during clearing, or as they washed dishes. They said I had fallen to the floor and begun convulsing violently. One had said a light had poured in from the pre-dawn darkness outside and had animated my unconscious body, she looked afraid as she remembered. Another said I had spoken the language of the angels but no one could tell me what I had said. Mostly the other women avoided me after this had happened.

When Mother Superior spoke to me, she said it was important that I realise the gift was not my own but that of humankind. She said I was merely the pigeon that carried the message to the world. I understood why she said this, it was to ensure I would not keep it jealously to myself and that I would not be destroyed by pride. Although this was her intention, what she said helped me in another way: it unburdened me. What I experienced felt more of an encumbrance than it ever did a gift; Mother Superior took away that weight and shared it between everyone evenly. After that day everything seemed to connect together in the convent. Every part of the schedule had its place and the organisation of the day pleased me. I did not have to think about what I would do next, it was all laid out for me, that way I could focus fully on the word of God.

As the winter months continued in the villa, my spirit became clearer. I walked like a spirit, parallel to the rest of the house, moving amongst them but in my own time and space. Between the Liturgy of Hours, study of the scriptures, and prayer and meditation, I would be in the garden. I found two abandoned vegetable beds towards the grotto in the villa's grounds I started to work the soil there each day, despite the midwinter frost turning the ground into rock. This is how my daily schedule remained until we were into the new year and the soldiers returned.[35]

---

35. Maybe what I'm forgetting is that Faith is a personal thing. Whether this document and the scrolls tell tale of the mistakes of mankind or not, it shouldn't stand in the way of this. The freewill imparted upon us is divine. I don't need to follow the mistakes of others. Tomorrow I'll start my own Liturgy of Hours and begin a fresh path to my own salvation.

X

Consilium

Whereas the early Vigils in the convent were my least favourite part of day, they were a blessing in the villa. There were two servants required to stay awake through the night. One was a member of kitchen staff who lit the ovens and made bread before the sun came up, to feed Lucius and the rest of the house when they awoke, and the other was the night servant who was at Lucius's beck and call, in case he needed anything. In truth, King Lucius generally slept well and, if he did wake, he went straight to Arthfael. There were some rare occasions when Arthfael would require the night servant's assistance, but usually Arthfael could sort most issues. The job of night servant was given to the most junior staff in the house because nobody liked to be up all night. There was not much actual work involved, but this made the night seem very long and tedious. To rise for Vigils in time, I asked the night servant, a pale young man, to knock on my door at four o'clock each morning. He would not open the door or speak to me; he would simply knock and walk on up the corridor. I would then dress and make my way to the Sacrarium. The villa was quiet at this time and I knew I would not see anyone. Once in the Sacrarium I would begin to read the Psalms aloud to myself. As I continued throughout the days, weeks and months, I started to feel my sisters at my side and Mother Superior's watchful eyes. I started to come to terms with the nights I had spent with Fagan beside me and was able to remember it with enough impartiality to pray for my soul and for the forgiveness I so desired. I also sought to understand and accept the loss of the gift. As Mother Superior had said, it was not my gift but a gift to the world. I was only a vessel in which the gift was carried until the time it was required. Now that the vital time had passed it was no longer needed. I was unburdened and free to live my life as a normal young woman.[36] By the time the men had returned

---

36. I've now officially moved to South Wales. I'm renting a small terraced house in Penarth and have taken a part-time job in a library in town. Most days I still

from the forests I had almost entirely disappeared into my own world, forgetting the importance of the baptised king and the missions to the villages. I had done my part. Now I could live out the rest of my life in quiet adoration of the Lord and allow those more qualified to integrate Christianity into the rest of Britannia. Fagan and Deruvian had other ideas.

It was during my precious, tranquil Vigils that I heard a clatter of hooves in the courtyard. A voice bellowed for the night servant. It was Deruvian, and I heard the sound of horses being led to the stables as

---

travel to the museum to study the scroll but I'm trying to reclaim my religion. And why should I let this nonsense get in the way of my belief?

... I'm not sleeping well. Despite rising before dawn each day, when I get into bed at night my mind will not switch off. Two nights ago, I think I must've drifted off sometime past midnight but I still felt awake. I must've been asleep though because I felt a cold wind across my face and saw the curtains shift and swirl. Then I could've sworn someone sat on the end of my bed. My feet felt pinned down by the blankets and I wanted to call out to ask who was there, but I couldn't. It was as though the air had been sucked from my chest. Once the feeling passed, my lungs expanded, and I gasped as big a breath as I could. My heart began to beat heavily and my bedroom seemed to move back into the present.

I got up early, as is my habit now, and read the Vigils and went to work. Although I had some spare time in the afternoon, something inside me could not face going to the museum that day.

I've been back once since but, no matter how hard I tried, I could not seem to concentrate on the writings. I left without saying goodbye to the curator and I've not been back since.

Regardless of my abstinence, last night I was visited again. Maybe it was another dream. It's possible that the stress of a brand-new direction in life, and the move, has all been too much and is culminating in waking nightmares.

I've been spending more and more time in church and the Vicar is helping me, though I cannot tell him everything of what I am going through.

Today, while putting a stack of books onto a shelf in the library, I felt a presence behind me, and then I heard someone breathe my name. When I turned to see who it was, predictably, no one was there. I couldn't shake the feeling all day, although as I sit here writing I feel alone again and I cannot decide if it feels good or a bad. I suppose it's mostly a sense of emptiness, which after a day of unknown surveillance is at least a welcome change if not a particularly pleasant one.

the men laughed and back-slapped their way inside. I read the Psalms a little louder, with more conviction, as my blood beat in my ears. When I reached Lauds, at six forty-five, the villa was at peace once again. The only noises were those I had become used to, the servants as they rose and went about their daily routine. After I had finished Terce it was time to eat breakfast. I crept from the Sacrarium and went to the kitchens to eat so as not to be caught in any riotous gathering of the king and his returning men.

That evening I felt pleased with myself for having avoided any contact with the household. I hoped they had forgotten me due to the excitement of their travels, their obvious victory, and their return to civilisation. After supper I returned to the Sacrarium and, just as Mother Superior had made us, knelt in private meditation as I did every evening. Somehow this practice did not feel as punishing when I decided to do it myself. About halfway through there were footsteps in the corridor. I chose to ignore them; I allowed the thud to flow around me but not disrupt my adorations of Jesus Christ. I did not turn to look but I could feel someone standing in the doorway. The footsteps had seemed too brisk to be Fagan, but I could smell blood. It was Deruvian, and, after he had waited a few moments to see if I would stop of my own accord, he apologised for interrupting and requested my company for a discussion with the king and Fagan. Without turning I told him it would be impossible as I had to finish the Liturgy of Hours and return to my chamber afterwards in order to rise before dawn. He chuckled and made a joke about being able to take the nun from the convent but not the convent from the nun, whatever that means. He told me that a peaceful outcome in the final village, Ciwa's village, would be easier to achieve with me by their side. He told me to think about it and then left.

For the next half an hour I searched my soul for an answer. I might have been naïve to the true nature of events that had rolled out after the baptism but I was not stupid. Even amongst the compliant villages I visited I could feel the resentment of the individuals. Their compliance had come at a price, a price that had been bargained during previous Roman contact. I had heard stories of Ciwa's village and had been shown some first-hand through the gift. If my gift truly was for all humanity, there must have been some reason why I had been shown. If there was any chance that my presence at Ciwa's village could prevent more human life fertilising the forest floor then I should attend. At least that is what I decided then. In truth, peace for the village was not an option they had even considered.

The last part of my tale describes my move from the world of the living. I have had great swathes of time to think about the events of the raid and to consider where I would have been had I continued my Liturgy of Hours that evening and gone to bed early. I could have left the men to do their job, and nothing would have been different for Ciwa or her village. The only alteration would have been that I would not have been there to die. I then wonder how my life would have played out. I would have left Britannia to return home. Maybe I would have died on the trip back; it was a dangerous trip. I might have made it back to the convent but died the year after of some disease or another. I might have lived many years in the convent to become Mother Superior as my sisters died around me. I might have lived until I was ancient and then died, having spent my entire life in the Liturgy of Hours. Would I have then transcended to heaven instead? I have exhausted a trillion possibilities but each time I come back to the same realisation: I was never meant to finish my Liturgy of Hours. Even if my presence at the village had not helped Ciwa and the women there, that I tried was enough to give myself some peace through eternity.

The men were around a table: King Lucius, Arthfael, Deruvian, and Fagan, with Adlais hanging onto his leg. As I entered, they stopped their discussion and Deruvian welcomed me with a smile. The king was excited, but Arthfael seemed downcast, dark rings under his eyes and he sat away from the others. I refused to look at Fagan, but Adlais muttered and gnashed her teeth as I joined the group. Deruvian pulled out a map and pointed to the area where Ciwa's village lay. They talked about how the compliance of this village would complete the conversion to Christianity in the area. With that area converted it was believed the rest of Britannia, which was generally under Roman rule, would be easy. The Roman records of Ciwa's village, however, were clear; an assault was not worth the loss incurred. There were notes that outlined the nature of the village, that as it consisted only of women, without outside influence it would eventually cease to be. As far as everyone was concerned, this was how the king's soldiers would handle them, by leaving them to their own devices. Fagan thought otherwise. The mission was complete, but without this final element resolved, to him it was unfinished.

Their plan was to pacify Ciwa, and with her pacification, the rest of the village would follow suit. Ciwa was the head of the wolf; cut off the head and the other women, who were normal women, would follow. My job, as a woman, was to go in with my books and convert Ciwa. Fagan and Deruvian were convinced I had already become firm friends with her during our visit and that she would be receptive to what I had to say. The men would stay out of the picture unless things became unsafe, as their presence, and especially the presence of any Roman soldiers, would create tension. I disputed the friendship they assumed I had formed but they assured me I would be fine. The idea of entering the village alone filled me with horror. As I spoke to Ciwa that day, I saw an outside innocence normally found in children or domestic animals, but what I saw inside was not of mankind or God. There was something I had not experienced before. That part frightened me, it was unpredictable. I think I knew she would show no interest in the scriptures, it was not her world, but the hope and faith instilled in me rose to the challenge. She must have been one of God's creatures, so God would speak to her when we needed him most.

We were to travel the very next morning; at the time I would ordinarily perform the Vigils. I lay awake for a while that night. I was afraid of Fagan returning to my room and I was also afraid of Ciwa. If I had not been so afraid to lose my own life, I might have seen the fragility of the proposed plan. The fact that they had spent months in brutality and were now talking of subtlety. If I had still had the gift, I might have seen what was coming sooner, and yet, I fear there may have been nothing I could do to change the outcome anyway. When I did drift into sleep, the room, again, was filled with the wintery forest as it had been before. This time, however, I was not pinned in place but free to roam. I walked through the snow and an excitement filled me and convinced me to run. I darted between the trees, so light on my feet. A pack of wolves came through the undergrowth and ran by my side. I was not afraid of them, they panted and howled, filled with joy. A knock at the door pulled me from my dream, it was four o'clock already. The anxiety I had for the day ahead flooded back into my body and my stomach gripped onto itself tightly.[37]

---

37. I have looked to the end of the scroll and found the part that corresponds with Tavia's story. This village is indeed described as Ciwa's Village in the original manuscript, but its eventual subjugation is documented in the same way as the other villages. This is with facts and figures of the number of soldiers that were lost, the number of inhabitants dispatched, and the subsequent spoils collected from the encounter. Amongst the four names of soldiers lost during this excursion is the name Tavia. No surname or job description, just the name Tavia. It is difficult to understand what she would've been doing there if you are to dismiss De Codine's script as pure fantasy.

XI

Mors Et Lupum

It had snowed overnight, and ice clung to the foliage of the evergreen trees. I travelled part of the way with Deruvian. He informed me of a second unit, that included Fagan and two or three other soldiers, but they would start later and join me in the village after I had time alone with Ciwa. Once we had ridden about halfway Deruvian stopped so I could ride on unaccompanied. He dismounted and gave me instruction on how to get to the village, and how to arrive with my life. He sat down and began to eat his packed breakfast and waved happily as I rode on alone.

Under the dense pine the forest floor was mostly snow-free but a thick hoar frost covered everything. The upper branches held deposits of flurries which sometimes dislodged in the breeze and glittered to the ground with a thump. I took a deep breath and filled my lungs with the brisk scent of trees and frozen needle-covered mud. Here, in this moment of peace and solitude, I stopped feeling afraid. A watery winter sun pushed its way through the canopy and shone shafts of gold around. Its beauty caused a tear to freeze down my cheek.

The closer I got to the village the more sense I had that someone watched. As Deruvian had told me, I dismounted after about an hour of steady riding and stood still to find my bearings. To my surprise, there was the faint smell of woodsmoke in the air and on the ground beneath me, I saw a dark patch where my horse had bled out in the first encounter with the villagers. A tingle of nerves caught up with me as I turned off the path and began to lead my horse towards where the smoke blew from. It seemed the breeze was behind the village, which made it easier for me to follow. As suspected, after I had walked for about fifteen minutes, a figure came out of hiding. There were no arrows or discussion, just a gesture to follow. They must have remembered my face from the previous visit.

I soon found myself in the clearing of the village, as if no time had passed. The snow lay thick on the ground and children played as the women went about skinning and butchering rabbits and collecting firewood to get them through the evening and night. I was taken straight to the largest roundhouse in the village, the home of Ciwa and her council.

The inside had not changed, dark and musty but somehow soothing. This time the wolves were up and about and bounded towards me as I entered. Ciwa barked at them, and they paused before me as their tongues licked at my hands. She remembered me, my friend Tavia, she said as she came over and wrapped her arms around my shoulders. Despite her size, she gripped me with incredible strength, and I gripped back, nervous that she would go too far and crush my bones. Ciwa seemed pleased I had come back to visit, it was, I imagined, how one might greet one's own sister after a long time apart. I allowed her to talk and to ask as many questions as she possibly could, some so specific it was almost impossible to answer: what time did I sleep until the day after we had first arrived at the villa? What was my favourite type of tree? What was Deruvian's favourite food? And how much did king Lucius weigh? She asked me what I had been doing at the villa, and as I knew the answer, I gave her as much detail as possible to steer her away from more difficult interrogations. She sat and listened, taking in everything I said and when, at last, I had to finish, she seemed satisfied and was quiet for a moment.

I relaxed. It was nice to talk to someone after the months of solitude but before I could feel too comfortable, she said, 'So you've come because you want us to be like you.'

It took me by surprise, not only that it seemingly came from nowhere but the way in which she worded the statement. I wanted to say no, that it was not entirely like that, but I could not. 'Yes, I suppose so,' I answered.

Ciwa then told me that the village had kept a close eye on how Deruvian and Fagan had moved through other settlements. Her manner had changed; she was focussed now and her voice did not betray her emotions in any way. She enlightened me on the way the men had subdued the hostile groups. There had been no attempt at conversion and there had been no survivors. One day they had gone to wash in the nearby stream, and it had turned red with the blood of their neighbours. Along the usual Bodunni hunting routes the soldiers had stuck heads on sticks: eyelids weighty, skin waxy and yellow, mouths wide in soundless screams. She told me of a woman who had been skinned, nailed up, and left to die and my mind moved back to that first encounter with these forests. I shivered and Ciwa put a fur blanket over my back.

I did not know what to say. I wanted to say sorry, that I had no idea, but I did have an idea. I knew enough about Deruvian and Fagan's souls to guess how the last free people of Britannia were dealt with. I chose to remain ignorant. The wolves got to their feet and began to sniff the air; Ciwa inhaled with them.

'Now it's our turn,' she said. She got up and began to gather her weapons. I told her it would not be the same way, that we had become friends, that Deruvian and Fagan had become their friends when we had visited. I told her I could help them convert and there need not be any deaths. But she said, 'No,' and, 'It's our turn, now.' She pointed to the door. I was confused until I heard the first shriek; it was not a cry of terror but one of rage.

I ran outside after Ciwa and saw a pregnant woman standing in the centre of the clearing. She was naked and her bare skin was caked with blood. In her hand was a small dagger and in front of her stood Deruvian, his tattooed chest and arms exposed to the cold winter air. I began to run towards him but before I had taken three steps the woman had lunged forward. He grabbed her and locked her arms around her back with one large hand while the other furiously stabbed holes into her body with her own dagger. He turned to Ciwa; he was almost unrecognisable to me, hair slicked back with sweat, face wild, and veins bulging from his skin.

The ground was already boggy with blood. Fagan and Deruvian had gone into the houses in silence and had rapidly slaughtered most of the women and children before Ciwa had sensed them. The wolves had not even noticed until the scent of the carnage began to seep into the room. Now I stood amongst it I could smell the butchery, like open bowels and rust The surviving members of the clan rushed from their huts to find soldiers entering the village to clear away any living Deruvian and

Fagan had not yet dealt with. The raid now descended into inevitable chaos and screeches of pain, but here we stood in the middle of the devastation, motionless. In this stillness I saw Deruvian's leg muscles twitch and I hurled myself between him and Ciwa. I moved with a speed and ease that I had never known and then felt something hit my chest with immense force, as if I had been punched hard. I fell to the ground, thinking someone must have thrown a large rock. I felt dizzy as I gazed up at the darkening dusky sky. Closest to the canopy was a dusty pink which faded into an odd green and then into rich indigo blue. The first stars emerged in the darkest parts. They glinted like tiny scraps of silver. A figure loomed over me and blocked out the last light. It was Fagan: he looked down at me and I smiled. It was a reflex, a pleasantry, it felt almost nice to see him again, familiar. He did not smile back. He pulled his sword from my chest and was gone. That is all I can remember.[38]

---

38. I found myself at Tinkinswood Burial Ground. I can hardly explain how or why. I followed the smell of rust and open bowels and discovered myself ankle deep in thick mud in the middle of a thundery shower of rain. The nearby river had burst its banks and I walked alongside its brown, fast-flowing waters until I saw a track that led towards a field, that led towards a narrow path, that took me to a stone retaining wall in herringbone pattern. Past the wall was the huge capstone roof of the chamber, which I crawled into and I lay down in the puddles that had stirred up on its dirt floors.

   As I lay there, the smell of massacre gave way to damp mossy stones and ammonia and the events of the past few months raced through my body to the sound of torrential rain outside. Something told me to stay there until I died. There was a darkness that crept into that place and tried to convince me that it would be better for everyone if I did not come back out.

   All I can think is that I'd experienced some kind of serious mental health breakdown.

   When I woke up it was night and I'd become very cold and wet. I thought I saw a light shine into the chamber, but as I crawled out I found nothing. The rain had stopped but the wind was icy.

   I must've been a sight, hair limp and tangled, clothes caked with mud, but as I walked up the side of the road a bus driver stopped on the way back to the depot. Despite it being the end of his shift, and me having not a coin to my name, he took me back to Penarth.

I was so grateful to him and he was nothing but courteous, but there was something about him that made me uneasy. He was probably in his thirties with a smile that was wide and mischievous. As I got off the bus near my house (I declined to tell him exactly where I lived) he told me to take care of myself and keep my hikes to daylight hours. He laughed as he closed the doors and the bus disappeared around the corner.

The whole experience has made me think hard about my health. I have decided not to continue my study with the scroll or indeed with this document and I will keep my faith the best I can.

Eleven

Tabitha woke up in her bedroom and curled up into a ball as she shivered. She looked over at her digital clock. It was five am and the floor had gone from beneath her bed to leave her afloat in an abyss. A darkness crept into her skull, sapped her body of energy, and caused her brain to lose its sense of balance. She buried her face in her covers and tried to go back to sleep. She put the feeling down to adjustment to a lack of alcohol or being pre-menstrual. Over the next hour the disorientation began to fade and as she warmed up she drifted off to sleep.

She opened her eyes again when the sun had come up. It was a little after nine on Christmas Eve morning and her mum had already left for work. Tabitha sat at the kitchen table and ate some cereal while she considered having a day off from adventure and intrigue in favour of not going out. However, some of the lethargy that harassed her of late had reduced and she felt better than she had for some time. She decided not to pass up the opportunity to use this energy to confront the situation and attempt to bring it to some conclusion. Whether that conclusion was good or bad didn't matter, she just wanted it to be done with. Maybe it could be as simple as returning the scrolls to the museum and keeping the key safe for her own next of kin one day.

Outside was fresh and, for the first time in at least a week, the sun shone. It occurred to her that the weather might have more influence on her mood than she imagined. She'd heard of a thing called Seasonal Affective Disorder; there was a woman on *This Morning* who had it and had been close to suicide on several occasions before being diagnosed. The only thing she needed to cure her was a UV lamp which she stared into for an hour a day, after that she was fine. The woman had shed a few tears and thanked her doctor who had come on the programme to explain the medical side of things and urge people to see their GP if they believed they might suffer from the same disorder. Since the woman's miraculous recovery she'd given birth to a beautiful baby girl and told the presenters her life was now complete. Everyone smiled, everyone was happy, the programme cut to an advertisement break.

Tabitha got on the bus. This time she had the document copy in her bag. She was confident that with all the troublesome objects together, she could tie up any loose ends, put the whole issue to bed, and move on with her life. Just as with Marguerite – she realised all she faced should have been obvious. The set up: that sense of hope that things were about to wrap up and everything would work out, the cheerful, despite unusual, behaviour of the boys the day before, *It's a Wonderful Life*. But the real world wasn't obvious. Actual events never followed simple decodable metaphors.

A smart BMW was parked outside Alex's house. She put this down to a visitor for a neighbour. She only took note because it was parked on the kerb over double yellow lines and she had to turn sideways to squeeze past. She knocked on the front door but was left waiting on the doorstep. She knew they were in, as she could hear voices. She heard Steven, though the words were quiet and muffled and she couldn't make out what was said. She then heard another voice, not Alex's; it sounded like an older man and although louder she still couldn't make out what he said due to the deepness of tone. As this continued inside, the shadows that had throbbed inside her before dawn began to return. Could the man be connected with the church? Maybe Alex had given the scroll to him. He could confiscate it and the ancestral chain of custodians would stop with Tabitha. The centuries of careful guard wrecked by her own erratic, threadbare character. Perhaps someone from the museum had found that the artefact had been taken and had reported it to the police. If she was caught stealing she would end up in prison this time. She could walk away – go back home. She could still revert to the original plan and forget the whole thing. Marguerite's document weighed down Tabitha's bag. Her shoulder felt strained and began to ache. She knocked again.

It was Steven who eventually answered. As soon as she saw his face it was clear things had gone wrong. His skin was red and puffy, and a look of despair segued to anger with the realisation that Tabitha stood at the door. As he commenced a bombardment of condemnation, she could tell he was himself again. Steven from the previous day had disappeared. She wasn't clear why he was so angry at first. He ranted, told her how it was all her fault, that Alex had been happy and normal until he met her. She tried to stop him to ask him what had happened but he would not listen and carried on his assault. When he started to get personal, calling her a nasty piece of work and throwing names at her like 'slut' and 'whore of Babylon', the older gentleman came to check what the commotion was.

'This is her!' Steven said. 'The one I told you about. She's the reason he did it!' Steven became more erratic and started to flail his arm in her direction as if he wanted to hit her but at the same time was too afraid. The older gentleman grabbed hold of Steven and gave him a soft shake before he escorted him back into the house. A few minutes later, after the shouting had died down, the man returned. At this point Tabitha stood frozen on the doorstep, too fearful to enter and too curious to leave.

'I'm terribly sorry about that,' the man said. 'I'm from the university.'

'What ... what's going on?' said Tabitha, now hoping for a story of Alex's expulsion but knowing it was something more.

'Your friend ... Alex ... he took his own life in the early hours of this morning.'

'Oh,' she managed to whisper. She wanted to react, to make some gesture of horror or grief. She wanted to slide to the floor with her hand tight over her mouth before a wail of anguish escaped into the sky. But she couldn't; she couldn't move. All she could do was say 'oh.'

The man had been one of Alex's lecturers and also his designated mentor. He invited Tabitha in and Steven went upstairs to his bedroom and slammed the door. The lecturer explained what had happened with tact and answered Tabitha's questions with soft tone. She learnt that Steven had found Alex in the bathtub at around six in the morning. Steven had thought there was a problem when he found the bathroom locked and received no answer when he called Alex's name. There was a nick in the lock on the outside of the door that meant it could be clicked open with a penny in an emergency. Steven did this and found his friend unresponsive, having cut his wrists and throat.

'He is, understandably, very shaken about the whole incident,' said the lecturer before he flattened his mouth and gave an empathetic nod towards her. 'He will get plenty of help from the university so don't worry.'

'I don't get it,' she managed, 'he seemed energetic yesterday ... confident like I've not seen him before.'

'That is not uncommon in this kind of situation. It's as though the final decision to end their life can create a calmness from the resolution even though they've been deeply unhappy before this point.'

'But he didn't seem unhappy,' Tabitha said, 'not really.'

'I know it's hard to take in,' he said as he put a kind hand on her shoulder. 'Steven blames himself, he said he should've recognised the signs,' he paused for a moment. 'Apparently Alex hadn't been sleeping well. Steven told me he had heard him up at all hours.' He paused again, this time for longer. Tabitha could see he was struggling with the situation himself. He floundered as he tried to decide how much information to divulge. 'He said Alex had complained that something was keeping him awake – a presence, like a heaviness in his room. He said it was sometimes hard to breathe.' He took his hand off her shoulder and dropped his gaze to the floor. 'I'm sorry ... it seems he might have been suffering from some serious mental health problems. I only wish we had noticed the signs sooner. I let him down.'

As the lecturer finished this last sentence there was a flurry and Steven re-entered the room. He threw the scroll directly at Tabitha. The fury and force behind his action caused the edge of the paper to cut her cheek. The scroll bounced from her and unwound itself across the floor. It was only a small scratch but as she scrambled to wind it back up a drop of blood fell onto the ancient paper. She was afraid the lecturer would see and start to ask questions and she would be implicated in Alex's death but he was busy restraining Steven. The lecturer walked Steven backwards towards the kitchen and attempted to soothe him. Once Tabitha had gathered the scroll into a loose roll, she shoved it into her bag and darted for the door while the two men were occupied.

At first she thought she would go home but decided to go straight to the museum, to return the artefact to the box. She had an expectation that Alex would text her – one of his apologetic texts – the whole thing being a misunderstanding or a joke. How often it happened that a character in a film would seem dead, only to stir and stand up to unleash the happy ending. Even ageless fairy tales, the princess in her tower or glass coffin. By this time bruised clouds had gathered over the sun, and as she sat at the front of the bus, she could hear excited voices on the driver's radio talking of a white Christmas.

'It'll never happen,' said an elderly lady, standing clinging to the rail as the bus came to her stop. 'We don't have snow like we used to, and when it does snow I feel it in my bones.'

The driver grunted as the bus came to a jolted halt and the doors hissed open. Tabitha got off too. There was a stop closer to the museum but she felt queasy and faint. Outside the temperature had dropped and the walk was uncomfortable. The cold air bit at her cheeks and dried her lips in an instant. The pavements were busy with midday Christmas shoppers, their hands filled with swollen carrier bags covered in festive designs. Tabitha weaved through the crowd and walked across the small park towards the museum building. As she approached she noticed through the windows that there were no lights on inside. 'No,' she whispered to herself and as she got closer, 'no ... no,' a little louder. On the door was a notice: 'Closed for Christmas' but she still pushed at the handle a couple of times and then kicked at the bottom with a strangulated screech. A homeless man sitting across the road glanced up and then looked away just as quickly. She calmed and sat down on the frozen stone steps at the front. She stayed for a while, mind blank, in the small hope that someone might come back and open up. After about half an hour she lifted herself and walked away with tentative steps and the odd glance back in case. She wandered the city centre, looking up at the decorations and admiring the large adorned tree, until she felt a chill right to her guts and found a bus that would take her back home. Despite the volume of people on the bus, with half the passengers having to stand, there was an air of joy. People offered their seats to others, even if they were not old or pregnant, and chatted to one another. At one point a box of mini mince pies was handed round. On a normal Christmas Eve she would have joined in with the merriment. Though she wasn't a typical candidate for Christmas cheer, it was the only time of the year she could lose her cynicism. It was also the time of year when you would visit houses and people would offer you alcoholic drinks, even in the morning. Brandy, port, sherry, and all sorts of fruity liqueurs were a warm and welcome way for her to float through the day.

She sat next to the window and watched the reflections of passengers as she picked up on snippets of their conversations, plans for the next day, and the things they had bought in town. She saw the ethereal outline of her own face, her own mouth downturned and the rings under her eyes. The bus emptied over a few stops and she was left almost alone with an unfathomable silence. The only sounds were the white noise that emanated from the driver's radio as it lost signal and the clicks from the indicators. There now came a moment when the world sank away and she was left suspended in nothing. She felt a lump grow in her ribcage and her chest ached as though she would go into cardiac arrest. At that point Tabitha thought that was it for her, that she had somehow lost her mind and her way and she would never live a normal life again. The driver then turned to a different radio station, which played carols from a service at King's College. The church organ resonated through the chasm to her and dragged her back to reality in time to see her stop pass by. She leapt up and pressed the bell and, although the bus had already gone past, the driver braked and let her off. He wished her a Merry Christmas as he fiddled with the radio again. *The Fairytale of New York* came on and he closed the doors and pulled away.

The house was empty and cold, so Tabitha went into the kitchen to turn on the boiler. On the table her mum had scratched in a note, 'sorry love no cover had to go back to work be back by 11.' Tabitha sighed. Her mum had said she would be home by midday so they could spend Christmas Eve together. On the counter sat a defrosting turkey that her mum had bought months in advance. It also looked as though she'd done another shop, probably after work that morning and before her extra shift. The fridge was stocked to the roof and the cupboards filled with all sorts of nuts, chocolate, and crisps. There was enough food for a family of five.

Tabitha changed into her pyjamas and dressing gown. She took the scroll out of her bag and put it on the kitchen table. She then went into the cupboard which they used to keep alcoholic drinks in before Tabitha drank too much and her mum stopped stocking up. She was thrilled to find one bottle of brandy and one bottle of port. She also went to the fridge and found a huge wedge of Stilton. Though her thoughts were on drinking until the murky misery of the day eased, she'd not eaten, and port was always better with snacks or cheese. She took the bottle, the cheese, and the scroll into the front room, collapsed onto the couch, and turned on the TV. She didn't bother to bring a glass or a plate; instead she swigged from the bottle and broke crumbled creamy chunks from the Stilton and stuffed them into her mouth. After she had flicked through a few channels of Christmas crafts, cooking, and crap, she found *The Muppets Christmas Carol*. It had been her favourite Christmas film when she was a child and it probably still was, something she wouldn't admit. Tabitha was absorbed in the story and her attention was drawn entirely to the bright puppets, a habit she hadn't grown out of. By the time the spirit of Christmas Present appeared she had begun to recite lines and, when she'd drunk about half the port, was laughing as she sang along. The film came to an end and the credits started to roll. The heavy alcohol mixed with her tiredness and she felt drowsy. As the adverts came on she drifted into a deep sleep.

Twelve

It was the first Christmas she could remember. Tabitha's parents had divorced by this point so the whole day was shared between her and her mum. When she woke up the sun hadn't yet risen and the house was filled with actual magic, not the kind of magic people described happiness and family as, but real magic that sorcerers and witches performed. She could hardly believe it was morning. When she'd gone to bed she couldn't fall asleep. There was a mix of anticipation and not wanting to miss the visit from Father Christmas. She was sure she would never be able to sleep as she rolled around in her bed and got her nightie caught around her midriff. Then – as if someone had wiped her memory – it was morning. Maybe Father Christmas had cast a spell to make her sleep.

She shuffled down the stairs on her bum, still in her nightie, with a feeling of excitement but also fear. What if the magical beings that had come were still around? She couldn't see any but there was substance to the air and the darkness seemed darker than usual. She reached up and clicked on the light with a sudden burst of colour and sparkle. There had been a few presents scattered under the tree the day before but now there was hardly any room for them all. They were wrapped in shiny patterned paper that glinted under the artificial light. On the mantle over the electric fire was the stocking she'd put up on Christmas Eve but now it was longer and bulged with all sorts of things. For a minute she was frozen in anticipation and thrill and as she tried hard to contain a shrill shriek of glee two arms came around her and scooped her up to reveal the smiling face of her mother.

'Go on Tabitha!' she prompted, 'see what Father Christmas has brought for you!' With that her mum put her down and Tabitha ran over to her stocking and pulled it down, spilling some of the contents over the carpet.

There was a myriad of pretty knick-knacks: mini-puzzles, plastic toys, a little teddy, a small picture book. However, she was most fascinated by the satsuma, tucked neatly in the toe of the stocking as if it had grown there; a bag of mixed nuts still in their shells, with walnuts crinkled like tiny brains; and a bag of coins that had either been minted with chocolate inside or transformed to have chocolate inside by an unknown force. Part of their appeal was how far they had travelled to get there. All the way from the North Pole. By eating them Tabitha thought she might absorb some wonder of that place. There was no doubt in her mind that it came from where she was told it had come from – there was no alternative explanation that would make sense.

As the watery winter sun painted the horizon it became apparent that it had snowed during the night. It wasn't deep – a light dusting of about half an inch – but it smudged the path and lawn outside into a fresh blank sheet and created a quiet that dominated the landscape. This perfect greeting-card scene created many damp, disappointing Christmas mornings in the future. That was until Tabitha got older and realised that a white Christmas was an exception rather than a rule. They ate breakfast facing the window and watched as now and then the wind blew a flurry down from the roof. The turkey was already in by this point, in a coat of bacon and under a blanket of foil, and the fan in the oven whirred as the heat radiated from the door into the chilly room.

After breakfast, Tabitha was allowed to open one present; the rest would wait until they had eaten dinner, washed up, and cleared the kitchen. Due to the rift in the family, most of the presents under the tree were from her mum. The others were from a work colleague and good friend of her mum's who was almost like a family member and another from Tabitha's aunty, her mum's sister, who they were still close with. Tabitha decided to open the present from her aunty. The paper was quite thin and tore easily as she slipped her fingers between the taped layers at the top. It probably wouldn't have mattered what was in the paper, Tabitha would have been excited anyway. Inside was a little set of gardening tools: a tiny rake, and a small trowel and fork inside a basket. Tabitha was so pleased with her present she insisted she should go out to use them. Her mum put her in her big coat, hat, scarf, and gloves and sent her into the back garden. There were no borders or anything to garden, so it was lucky it had snowed as Tabitha was able to scoop and rake at the light powder and trowel it into her basket. After about an hour her mum came out and made her go back inside. The sky had clouded again, and the temperature had dropped, though Tabitha had been unaware as she busied about her important job. She only felt cold once she got back into the house. Her fingers and toes were red and her nose began to run as soon as the heat warmed her face. Her mum took Tabitha's coat off and sat her at the table while she made some warm Ribena. They sat together, Tabitha with her squash and her mum with a cup of black coffee. They shared a mince pie between them and a slice of Christmas cake.

Before dinner Tabitha watched *The Snowman* on television. She cried a bit when the choirboy sang *We're Walking in the Air* – not because of the story but because the song sounded sad. When the snowman melted at the end, she was disappointed but not upset. Soon her mum called for her to turn the TV off and come to the table. When she got to the kitchen, she saw the dining table had been covered with a red tablecloth and there were two tablemats with a knife, a fork, a spoon, and a cracker beside each. Tabitha climbed onto her chair and waited for her mum to finish preparing the food. Instead of dishing it onto the plates like she usually did, today she put the vegetables on the table in bowls and the turkey in the middle on a big platter and put an empty plate onto each tablemat. To Tabitha's delight her mum then dished the food onto her plate in front of her, asking her how much she would like. By the end her plate was filled like it had never been before, and her mum asked her if she thought she would be able to eat it all. Tabitha nodded sullenly and her mum replied with, 'I think your eyes might be bigger than your belly!' Before they started to eat, they pulled crackers. Tabitha's mum read out the jokes and they laughed as they put on their paper hats.

The radio was on and played a stream of carols as they ate. At times Tabitha's mum would purr the words in the choruses. Their images of ships, wise men, deep snow, and fields of sheep permeated the room while Tabitha ploughed through her meal. It was as though she walked through scenes on Christmas cards that covered the walls and mantlepiece. The cold snow crunched under her feet, she smelt the lamb wool, and tasted a salted wind whipped up from the ocean. Her tiny hands worked away at the meat on her plate and the stuffing, which she left until last because she liked it the most.

When they had finished her mum cleared away the dishes as she sat still. The volume of food had stretched her tummy out and made it ache. She pulled up the bottom of her T-shirt and saw her bellybutton, deeper than usual. When her mum asked if she wanted pudding she thought she wouldn't be able to fit it in but she didn't want to wait until later or miss out altogether. Tabitha nodded and her mum brought over a small bowl of Christmas pudding with custard. Tabitha had never tried Christmas pudding before and she found the taste heavy and bitter in places despite the sweetness of the custard. She didn't like it much but as she'd asked to have some, she didn't want to disappoint her mum so ate everything.

Tabitha sat motionless as her mum finished clearing the dishes. Tabitha thought she would be sick if she moved. She was right. After everything was tidy, they went into the front room to open the rest of the presents. With the added excitement of what was under the tree, Tabitha felt everything she'd eaten rise in her throat as if it had nowhere else to go. Then, as she clamped her fingers over her mouth, a great geyser of undigested dinner spurted onto the carpet. Her mum, who had been getting the presents out, raced towards her at the same second, scooped her up by her armpits, ran upstairs to the toilet, and plonked her down in front of the bowl. At this point it was too late, there was enough space made in her tummy for the rest of the food in there to sit comfortably. Tabitha lay curled on her bed for a bit while her mum sorted out the mess. She felt guilty but fell into a light sleep and dreamed she opened her present which turned out to contain an elephant.

Later, after she'd recovered, Tabitha went back downstairs and they finished opening the presents. After this Tabitha had a glass of pop and they watched some Christmas television. As the sun set, and Tabitha's mum went round the house drawing the curtains, Tabitha felt sad. She didn't want the day to finish; not just the day but the whole run-up to Christmas. They would take the decorations and lights down and the toys and pretty things in the shops would go, then they would be left with winter. They would have leafless trees, grey skies, and cold dark mornings. When Tabitha's mum got back downstairs Tabitha was crying. She sat down, put Tabitha on her lap and wrapped a blanket around the both of them without asking her what was wrong. That is where Tabitha went to sleep.

When Tabitha woke up there were bits of Stilton smeared into her top and her mouth felt sticky and dry from the port. She took another swig from the bottle as her eyes focussed on the television. A man was talking on the news, but his voice was louder, closer, and deeper than it should be. The sun had gone down and the heating had turned off while she slept. The room was frigid and dim apart from the light of the screen, which glittered on the branches of the unlit tree. The room was paler, the furniture and carpets washed out in the night. Tabitha shivered and wrapped her dressing gown tighter. The scroll had folded into the gap between her and the edge of the seat and she pulled it out and stuffed it into her pocket. She tried to make sense of what was being said but the words didn't match the movement of the lips, and when the newsreader changed the voice stayed the same. There was a clip of a field and the countryside and someone spoke about a chariot burial. This was news because they hadn't thought chariot burials were performed in Wales. Chariot burials were reserved only for nobility. Tabitha was motionless, sitting upright in her chariot sunk deep into the ground and covered to travel to the next world. She was still groggy and half-cut but as her awareness returned dread crept up her arms and legs and into her chest.

During her GCSE year Tabitha had found herself under stress for the first time. Her teachers would call her to one-to-one meetings on a regular basis to give her the same spiel about potential she had and potential she wasted. She knew she wasn't stupid but it was more fun to lounge through break with her friends in an acrid cloud of weed smoke and giggle through the afternoon on the creaking back legs of her chair in a class that was too easy. Unlike her friends, though, she wasn't good at being ignorant. Her mind would catch onto an idea and rerun the image like a snapped piece of film. Just before they broke up for Christmas, in the year of her GCSEs, they were shown a video about the homeless. It was a clear attempt by the school to turn them into sympathetic caring members of society and it did succeed at first to make Tabitha think of those who have nothing. The video followed the story of three or four homeless people during the winter period. They told their stories and explained how tough it was on the streets. One particular young woman had more time on screen. She'd been put into prostitution by her father at a young age and had been controlled by her pimp with crack cocaine. The young woman escaped to a different city but now lived on the streets where she was regularly assaulted both sexually and physically. She spoke of her hopes and dreams in life and urged people not to waste their chances. After the credits had finished, a message came up informing the viewer that after completion of the film the makers of the documentary learnt that the young woman had died on the coldest night of the year after she'd been raped and beaten unconscious. It also said, before the screen went black, that the police had no leads and were not pursuing the case. The students were silent for a moment and as the teacher went to turn the television off a final photo flashed up. It wasn't the usual smiling memorial photo with a date beneath, but the photo of her dead body in an alley that the police had taken. It was only up for a second before the teacher, who had trusted the age certification of the film and not checked it personally, switched it off with moist eyes from both sadness and alarm. She then tried to gloss over the finale but there was a fear in her voice that suggested she might be in trouble if any sensitive children told their parents.

Afterwards Tabitha joked about it with her friends – insensitivity was an important part of their group dynamic – but in reality the image was burned onto her retinas. When she lay in bed that night she could see the twisted frozen nude woman like a hung pig carcass. She could see every wound and purple bruise crystallised by frost in sharp detail as if the picture was in front of her. A door had opened that wasn't only locked before but somehow hadn't existed. Now she could see inside, there was an infinitely huge room that was darker than any darkness she thought possible. That was when she started to have visions and nightmares of her own frozen death: in alleyways, beneath the ice of a lake, on top of snow-capped mountains, and deep in the Arctic with toes and parts of her face bitten off by frost. She began to believe every choice she'd made would lead her to an early grave and saw the teachers had been right about her GCSEs. Unfortunately there wasn't enough time to catch up and all of her cramming and studying only led to acute heart palpitations and anxiety attacks which left her breathless and afraid she would die right then and there. Her mind at this time unravelled more than she thought possible. There was another part of her that observed from afar and told her that even if she didn't die immediately she could end up committed. When she failed her GCSEs and finished school, the fear of the abyss of death and panic attacks eased. Her mum supported her and helped her realise that failing her GCSEs wouldn't mean the end of existence. However, Tabitha had seen how brittle her mind could be and that worry never left.

Tabitha's brain had become exhausted. Maybe she had used too many drugs and drunk too much and this was her fate but she wasn't confused and felt aware. This wasn't how she imagined a psychotic episode would feel, but maybe that was what made them dangerous. She got to her feet and took some deep breaths, and although the dread remained there was no panic. She turned off the television and the room fell into further gloom. She could still hear the voice – it was a deep gravelly voice and now spoke in a language she didn't know. From her time with Alex she deduced it sounded like Latin, but she couldn't be sure. She went to the wall next to the kitchen to turn on the light but there was no switch. She checked on the other side of the door in case she'd somehow got it wrong but found the wall smooth and bare. The floor crunched beneath her feet as she moved to the front door, all the time taking long steady breaths. She wouldn't let this get the better of her – she would go to the neighbours and calmly ask if they could call her mum or an ambulance. She opened the front door and closed it behind her and as she turned found herself in a field. Now comprehending that it had been a mistake to leave the house, she spun on her heel to get back in but found the door gone. The whole house was gone.

'Well,' she said to anyone who would listen, 'I suppose I left a while ago.'

Thirteen

It was a bitter night. The temperature had dropped below freezing and a wind had begun to whip across Wales from the east. Tabitha's face felt stiff and her nose and lips dry from the chill that cut through her dressing gown and pyjamas. As she'd only planned to go next door, she'd not put her shoes on. The frozen mud felt as though it would slice through the bottom of her feet as she stumbled and stubbed her toes. She didn't know where she was going, just that if she kept walking she could stay warmer and come to a road or a landmark at some point. She checked her dressing gown pockets for her phone but only found the scrolls and her lighter, which she always kept in there. She remembered the row she had with her mum the first time she tried to smoke in the house. It had been another nippy night and Tabitha wanted to stay in but her mum said it was disgusting and would make everything in the house smell disgusting. Even as Tabitha argued her case, she knew her mum was right and equally didn't want the house to smell. From then on Tabitha would go in her dressing gown and sit on the plastic patio furniture when she wanted a cigarette.

Tabitha could still hear the muttering in Latin over the howl of the wind. She managed to make her way across the field to a hedgerow where a flock of sheep sheltered. As she stumbled forward they bolted and bleated in shock and their hooves drummed against the hard ground as they followed a thin path across the expanse. Tabitha watched the white ghostly forms as they bounced away and vanished. She thought if she followed the hedges she would be more likely to find her way somewhere and the vegetation would act as a windbreak. When she got there, however, she found the hedge had protected the ground from the frost and the mud there was soft and filled with sheep shit that squidged between her toes. It also hid debris from the trees and hawthorns, which she found out as a long spur sank deep into the ball of her foot. Her feet had become icy enough that she couldn't feel the pain but she thought of the germs that were now stuck under her skin.

The sky was clear and sprayed with stars. There was an almost full moon which allowed Tabitha to see where she was going to some extent. The pale light sparkled off the forming frost on the ground and took Tabitha's attention for a short time, bringing her to the present which fired her determination to get back home. The wind dropped for a moment and as it did so the murmuring Latin in the background also softened. She thought she might be recovering, until she turned a corner and the voice became louder again. She spun round and found it quieter. Without anything else to go on she decided to follow the voice which now drew her across the centre of ploughed ground. Her ankles rolled as she stumbled through the troughs and peaks that seemed carved from the earth like furrows in a sculpture.

After at least half an hour of this Tabitha tripped and landed on her knees. She felt tired and the confusion that had been absent before crept into her head. She rolled onto her back and looked up at the sky while the voice that had whispered before now boomed around her and reverberated in her skull. The wind ripped through branches and the sound of a fox's shriek carried through the broken air. For a moment her heart pushed harder. She could hear the throb of her blood in her ears and a warmth thrust into her petrified fingers and toes. Her head cleared and the Latin was cut through by a woman's voice. The voice sounded layered, like a choir, voice upon voice, the same voice but different depths – the depth from age with the oldest being the deepest. The voice said, 'Tabitha,' and as she pulled herself up onto her feet again, she joined in. 'Come on, Tabitha,' she said.

Though the original speech hung in the background, this new chorus eclipsed it and drew her towards it with renewed energy. Tabitha soon reached a low fence with barbed wire on top. She put her foot about halfway up the fence and – holding the top with her hands between the barbs – managed to swing her other leg to the opposite side. Now straddling, she pulled over her other leg with care and stepped onto the short grass. As she walked away she heard the rip of her dressing gown which had caught. Now tattered, she moved on through the night and saw an odd place sign sticking out cf a bramble patch. She went up and took the lighter out of her pocket so she could make out what it said. *TINKINSWOOD BURIAL CHAMBER* she read and beneath it in Welsh *SIAMBR GLADDU TINKINSWOOD*. There was a white arrow pointing up a path and as the flame went out she realised why she was here – though wondered why she couldn't have found herself in front of the sign after walking through her front door rather than in a footbath of cowshit.

The grass around the burial ground was kept low for visitors and closer to the site was another sign with maps, diagrams, and histcrical facts. Tabitha didn't bother to read them as the choral med.ey had increased in volume and had been joined by other monologues in a multitude of languages and tones. As she walked past a retaining wall of herringbone stonework, she caught sight of the large capstone over the chamber. When she approached the structure a cloud rolled in front of the moon and across the richly starred sheet above. The wind moved off into the distance but cooler air came in behind it and she could see her breath even in the dimness. She blew on her hands and plunged them into her pockets as she advanced and ducked into the chamber that looked as if it had been plonked there by giant Neolithic children. The voices all stopped at once and she was left in a silence that filled her every cell and softened the muscles in her body. Inside, out of some of the weather, it was a degree or two warmer. There was the smell of piss and an old Stella can lay crumpled to the side. She sat away from the side in the dusty dirt and put her head in her hands. She felt the age of the stones try to speak to her. They told her stories of their history and of the bones that had been laid to rest. She felt the presence of Tavia and Gueraula de Codines – or whatever her fuck.ng name was – prompting her to join them in their soap opera across time and space. Fagan was there too, she could feel his heavy bitterness, and his jester, Deruvian, as a wingman in war crimes. And there, sitting in her lungs, was the last true king of Wales. Lucius I. He was still insane with regret that his own son had fucked it up. They all wanted a piece of her, to use her like her ancestors and Marguerite, so that she could somehow perpetuate their squabble into eternity. She took a deep breath and thought of Alex. Maybe when the Romans came to Britannia life was cheap. People only lived to their thirties, and most of your children dying was a given, but that wasn't how it was now.

Tabitha pulled herself onto her haunches and shuffled towards the entrance of the chamber. There she pulled the scroll from her pocket. It was smeared with mud but as she held the lighter to it the fat from the stilton began to catch alight in one corner. Once the flames had crept higher, she threw it out into the night and watched the orange glow take hold. She sat back against the stones and felt their coolness seep into her back. The voices and feelings started to soak away into the earth underneath. As she watched the flicker she felt herself soothed into a peaceful sleep, and as her eyes closed the first flake of soundless snow twisted through the night and landed on the burning scroll. Before a minute had passed the blaze was smothered under a thin blanket which thickened with increased flurries.

Appendix

Account of the events leading up to the dictation of the hagiography of St Fagan as written by Gueraula de Codines's travel companion, Martina de Baylen. Translated from the original old Castilian.

We reached the Welsh marches whilst England writhed in the depths of civil war. The border lands were strewn with fortifications but we slipped in unchallenged, no soldier bothered by the presence of two women of Castile travelling alone. Had we been French it may have been different. My mistress, Gueraula de Codines, had been personally requested by the wealthiest and most powerful marcher lord, Hugh Despenser the younger. The name of the Divinatrix de Parrochia de Subirat had travelled far beyond Subirat. Stories of her miraculous healing abilities in all creatures and blindingly accurate fortunes had reached the shores of England. Had it not been for Gueraula de Codines, I myself would be bound to my bed, my spine twisted into great distortion by all manner of malevolent spirits.

Hugh Despenser the younger and Edward II were close. Before Gueraula de Codines had been requested, a huge amount of land in England and Wales had been returned to Hugh Despenser the younger following great conflict amongst the Lords of the Marches. Hugh Despenser the younger had a great many powerful enemies but it was his wife, Eleanor de Clare, who was paying the price. However, as we left Castile we were unaware that Eleanor de Claire was the reason for our travel. The request given to Gueraula de Codines described a disease that had run rampant amongst the horses of the kingdom and had spread to dogs and some stable workers. The result was a mass of ulceration around the victim's head and mouth initially, then spreading to the rest of the body, coughing, fever, a hideous discharge from the nose, and eventually death. This disease spread from animal to animal with great ease and the sky had become thick with smoke from the fires lit to destroy the poisoned carcasses. When we set foot on the long-disputed isle, autumn was moving swiftly into winter, and the frosty mists mixed with the sickly smell of burning beasts.

Eleanor de Claire was not suffering from the plague of the horses. She, of course, had been kept away from any diseased souls. Her predicament was altogether rather more strange. When we entered the house of Lord Hugh Despenser, we were taken to the Lady's bedchamber. There she lay perfectly motionless, her eyes staring wildly at the ceiling. We were told that she had been this way for more than a month. She'd not eaten and had only drunk a little water each day, which her handmaid trickled into the Lady's slightly parted lips. She had become thin and pale, her chestnut locks fell out by the handful, replaced by thin white wisps of hair. Gueraula de Codines asked the Lord if anything had happened to her before this change, and he told her that it had not. Here the handmaid looked down at her feet, a picture of distress on her face. I noticed this and asked her if she knew anything. She looked up at the Lord. 'Sir?' she said. He told her that if she had any information, she should share it with us.

This was when we first heard his name. The handmaid told a story that had begun with the innocent research of the Lord and Lady's home. The Lady had happened to uncover documents within the closest church that had associated the land on which their house had been built to an ancient royal bloodline. Excited by her findings, the Lady dug deeper and found bound Latin volumes, written by the Roman occupation, which described the movement from pagan sin to Christendom. It seemed this move had been led by a small group of missionaries sent from Rome, their head being Fagan and his companion Deruvian. Within these volumes, which, due to the Lady's status were gladly interpreted for her by a monk, were described the first baptism of a native king, the peaceful conversion of the settlements that would eventually become Wales, and most importantly the miracle. It was written that the decapitated head of St Alban had appeared to them during the baptism of Lucius, despite Alban not being martyred until at least the 3rd century. Convinced that she had found the hagiography of a saint of whom, at this point, very little was known, the Lady Eleanor de Claire took these texts from the church in order to send them to Rome.

The night before she was to send them, the handmaid awoke to a scream in the Lady's bedroom, adjacent to her own. She hurried in and found Lady Eleanor de Claire now breathless and crimson as if choking beneath some invisible weight. The handmaid described the room as being blacker than she ever thought possible. Its thickness even muffled the light from her candle. The handmaid attempted to lift the Lady in order to sit her up against the head of the bed but found her to be like lead. The handmaid now saw the volume that the Lady had taken from the Church, open and creased on the floor. Without fully understanding why, she had picked up the volume, closed it, and hid it under a loose floorboard in her own room. When she re-entered the Lady's chamber the surrounding darkness had become natural again. Eleanor de Claire had gone quiet and had returned to a more normal pallor though was still not herself. Considering now that the Lady had been under the weight of some supernatural might, the handmaid decided to keep the incident a secret for fear that the Lady's reputation may be tarnished by talk of punishment from God.

At this point we were taken into the handmaid's room and shown the volume that she had hidden. After Gueraula de Codines briefly examined the writings, Lord Despenser had it immediately taken from the house, though at the time we had not known where. The revelation had not eased Lady Eleanor de Claire's condition at all so Gueraula de Codines set about her work trying herbs, powders, prayers, and leeches in any attempt to bring the poor woman from her frozen state. Nothing succeeded, and Lord Hugh Despenser was becoming irascible. Then, three nights after we had arrived, Gueraula de Codines had a vision. She told me only a few details of her vision, that she was standing amongst pine trees, their branches weighed down with snow. She saw two women, one that suckled from the teats of a wolf and darted through the undergrowth as a great thunderstorm raged in the distance, and the other a nun, in religious habit. It was the nun that spoke and told her that resolution would come from a visit to a nearby burial chamber of the ancients between the hours of midnight and one.

Late the next day, December 18th 1325, we travelled to the site of the burial chamber that was only an hour away by horse. We were lucky the stable still had a number of horses untouched by disease. During the next three nights the book was dictated to Gueraula de Codines. After the dictation was completed we returned to the house and found Lady Eleanor de Claire entirely herself. Lord Hugh Despenser attributed this not to Gueraula de Codines' labours, but to his own actions of sending the guilty manuscript away to Rome to be examined by the Pope's own clerics. Due to this, Gueraula wasn't paid, and penniless, all we could do was return to Castile.

To reveal the secrets we have learnt and speak out against a saint of the Catholic church would be suicide so Gueraula de Codines has hidden the dictation until, what she describes as, a day when truth is worth more than self-serving deception.

Postscript:

A year after my and Gueraula de Codines' departure from Wales, we heard tell of Lord Hugh Despenser the younger's swift downfall and gruesome death following the ruin of King Edward after the nobility had rallied to an invasion from France rather than siding with King Edward and the Despensers. By many accounts Lord Hugh Despenser had tried to starve himself before his trial but failed. He was found guilty of treason, stripped naked, and dragged through the streets. They said his body appeared to be printed with unknown Latin documentation. Some believed his torturers had done this, that they were Bible verses that described the sins he had committed. However, there was speculation that it was already there when they had removed his clothes and some scholars present said that they were not bible verses at all but seemed to be descriptions from Roman rule in early Britannia. The executioners then hanged him, but took him down before the point of asphyxiation. After which they tied him tightly to a ladder, burned his genitals, and castrated him. He then came to his grisly end when he was sliced open and relieved of his internal organs.

For many years Gueraula de Codines has kept her ear to the ground, listening for any revelations about Saint Fagan. She listened for signs from monasteries, convents, churches, and amongst her more wealthy and religious patients but has heard nothing. She believes the Roman writings never made it to the Vatican.

* * *

The sound was something like polystyrene crushed against a heavy boot but muffled as if she were underwater. There was a scent like spicy autumn leaves mixed with ammonia and a numbness deep into her hips and legs. She tried to move but her limbs felt as if they were filled with sand. The sound changed to a clunk, shush, clunk, shush, which continued for a few minutes until a new clarity hit her ears as if she had surfaced. She then heard her name but this time the voice was there with her, not echoed through time.

'Tabitha?' it said again. She managed to prise her eyes open only to squint them back shut when a light shone into her face. She felt arms wrap around her chest and begin to haul her from the dirt and onto a prickly cushion of snow. The sudden change in temperature made her gasp and shook awake her extremities. It was still night and as she came to she saw the outline of a figure holding a torch. She already knew, before the figure shone the torch towards its face and said, 'it's me, sweetheart,' who it was. She also knew that the tone would change from 'are you okay?' to 'what on earth were you thinking?' in a few short moments.

'What day is it?' Tabitha mumbled into her mum's shoulder as they walked to the car.

'It's okay,' she replied, 'you haven't missed it.'

Milton Keynes UK
Ingram Content Group UK Ltd.
UKHW032151260924
448786UK00005B/352

9 781789 634228